"Ski with me, or your life ends right here ... right now!"

Karen swallowed hard. Time. She desperately needed time—to think.

She surveyed the perilous trail below. Her heart pounded, her tongue dried up in her mouth so she could hardly swallow. Snow was falling, fast and thick. She could barely see twenty feet ahead of her ski tips. *This is the last I'll know of the world,* she thought. *Cold ... crashing down a mountainside ... sailing off into the sub-zero air for a second or two before crashing down onto jagged rocks!*

"No more stalling! ... move!"

Avon Books are available at special quantity discounts for bulk purchases for sales promotions, premiums, fund raising or educational use. Special books, or book excerpts, can also be created to fit specific needs.

For details write or telephone the office of the Director of Special Markets, Avon Books, Dept. FP, 1350 Avenue of the Americas, New York, New York 10019.

Winterkill

Nicole Davidson

AN AVON FLARE BOOK

WINTERKILL is an original publication of Avon Books. This work has never before appeared in book form. This work is a novel. Any similarity to actual persons or events is purely coincidental.

AVON BOOKS
A division of
The Hearst Corporation
1350 Avenue of the Americas
New York, New York 10019

Copyright © 1991 by Kathryn Jensen
Published by arrangement with the author
Library of Congress Catalog Card Number: 91-91773
ISBN: 0-380-75965-9
RL: 6.0

First Avon Flare Printing: July 1991

AVON TRADEMARK REG. U.S. PAT. OFF. AND N OTHER COUNTRIES, MARCA REGISTRADA, HECHO EN CANADA.

Printed in Canada.

UNV   10   9   8   7   6   5   4   3

FOR NICOLE—
a daughter as beautiful and
full of dreams as
the mysterious
opal

Prologue

Karen Henderson wrapped her arms around her body and shuddered. Her long blond hair hung in a tangled mess around her cheeks. Mascara had streaked around her soft amber eyes, which were swimming in tears.

Still wearing her ski jacket, she sat in front of the fire that blazed in the huge stone fireplace, but her bones felt as cold as a tombstone. She'd been sick twice—once before the police arrived, once after. She thought she might throw up again, except she was empty.

This can't be happening to me! *she thought through her exhaustion.* Healthy people don't die at seventeen! Not people I know!

But she'd seen the body: eyes dead and staring, blood-smeared and battered flesh. And she'd been there—oh, God!—she'd watched it all happen, so she couldn't deny it was true. Her closest friend in this tiny town had just been wiped off the face of the planet. And there had been nothing—nothing!—she could have done about it.

Or was that really true? Hadn't she received more than one warning? Reflexively, her hand reached up to clutch the fragile glass bauble hanging from a gold chain around her throat.

"Karen," a disembodied voice called.

She shivered in response and tightened her fingers around the necklace, squeezing her eyes shut. Just leave me alone, *she silently begged.* For God's sake, go away!

"Karen, I'm sorry. This can't wait any longer. I've already spoken to all of your friends. It's your turn."

She could feel the other kids from her school—sitting mutely, in clusters or alone, around the lounge— watching her, waiting for the police to tell them they could go home to their own beds to sleep off a nightmare of a party.

Wearily, she shook her head. It felt as if something had come loose up there, like a couple of plastic dice rattling around in the cardboard shaker when she played Liar's Dice with her friends.

A warm hand rested on her shoulder. "Karen, look at me."

Obediently, she gazed up at the Vermont state cop. He was in full uniform but had removed his hat. His face glowed a demonic orange in the flickering firelight. After a moment, she realized his beard-stubbled cheeks actually were a pulpy gray; deep lines around his eyes and mouth revealed his fatigue.

"I . . . I can't." She choked helplessly as steamy *tears began to flow down the back of her throat again.*

"It's important that I get a complete statement from you while everything's fresh in your mind, before you forget details."

I'll never forget tonight! *she thought miserably.* Never in a million years.

Every horrible second was indelibly fixed in her brain. The lights hovering in the darkness approaching

2

faster, faster. The screams of terror. And, after what seemed like an eternity in hell, the sight of a living person being mangled into a limp pulp. A person, someone she'd cared deeply for, had been transformed before her eyes into an almost inhuman form that, however impossible it might seem, could still call out her name and reach for her in the night.

Breaking into sobs, Karen began to tremble uncontrollably.

"Karen," the police officer squatted in front of her, his strong fingers ringing her upper arms, giving her a gentle shake, "don't collapse on me now. I need you, honey. You're the only one who was close enough to see anything. Tell me what happened. If you think you know who did this, tell me."

"And then what?" she asked weakly. "Nothing will bring my friend back."

"You're right," he admitted, staring into her tear-filled eyes for a moment. Then his mouth stiffened, and his face took on a dark, very uncoplike expression of vengeance. "But maybe you and I can nail the bastard!"

Yes, she thought with a flicker of hope. *Oh, yes!*

So she started at the very beginning and told him everything she knew.

Chapter 1

January

It was the scariest day of her life—a bright, white winter morning that was to be her first day at Killington Regional High. Karen Henderson stepped out of the shiny, dark blue convertible she'd received for her sixteenth birthday, which still wore its New York plates. She glared dismally at the low brick building nestled among acres of tall pine trees.

"Whatever possessed them?" she muttered to herself. "They must have been insane." She was thinking of her parents, of course.

Only a few months earlier, Karen had been blissfully unaware that her mother and father were plotting to ruin her life. Their Manhattan apartment had been her home for as long as she could remember. It was spacious and glitzy, full of modern furniture and art nouveau prints in soft pastels and gold frames.

Her father's obstetrical practice had loaded her bedroom with everything a teenage girl needed to be happy—a state-of-the-art rack stereo system including CD changer, a walk-in closet jammed with clothes from her favorite shops (Carmen's on East 34th was her favorite), her pet parakeet Romeo, and a zoo full of stuffed animals she'd collected since her toddler days.

Her friends were sophisticated and shared her interests. On weekends they went out clubbing together, had brunch, shopped, shopped, and shopped some more. The Big Apple, New York City, was her *world*, and she loved it. *Loved it!*

Then her parents decided to "get back to nature." As if they'd ever been there before.

"Darling," her father explained one tragic Sunday afternoon, "there's more to happiness than personal possessions and chasing the almighty dollar."

"Just think of the simple joys of pine-scented air and freshly baked bread," her mother chimed in, flashing her daughter a delirious smile.

"What about my friends?!" Karen wailed in disbelief.

"I'm sure they'll be dying to come up to Vermont for a visit."

"Sure!" Karen moaned. "For spring break . . . a weekend of skiing maybe. Once a freaking year!"

The rest of the time she'd be stuck in the boonies with a bunch of hicks. Vermont. All she could visualize were red-and-black checked lumber jackets and sensible wool caps with ear flaps. They probably didn't even have cable yet!

So here she was, despite her wildest protests. The truth was, she really had no options. No relatives existed with whom she could move in, not since her grandmother died last summer. And none of her friends' parents in the city would be willing to put her up for more than a week at a time. On the other hand, she wasn't so stupid she'd seriously consider striking out on her own. She'd seen how runaways

6

ended up, in spite of their exciting dreams—in squalor and fear, sleeping on subway grates beneath sheets of cardboard.

On a woodsy hillside in Killington, Vermont, her father established his medical practice in the basement of a drafty two-hundred-year-old house that cost a fortune to renovate. Her mother gleefully experimented with baking old New England specialties— deep-dish apple pie, Indian pudding, baked beans with molasses, and steamed brown bread. Some of the results were even edible. And Karen waited nervously for the end of Christmas break—to start school.

Now, glancing down at her hips with apprehension, Karen tugged on the loose sweater she wore. The weather wasn't really warm enough to go without a jacket, and she was cold standing outside in the January wind. But she could probably get away with wearing the sweater inside, and it was sufficient camouflage for the ten pounds she'd gained since her parents announced their master plan. It seemed as if all she'd done from that day forward was stuff her face.

Tenderly, she patted the flawless midnight blue hood of her little car. At least some things hadn't changed. She still had her wheels, her ticket to freedom. If life got too boring she'd take off for a weekend and drive back to the city; any one of a dozen of her friends would put her up for a night or two.

With a sigh, Karen locked up her car and headed for what appeared to be the front of the school. A couple of buses were unloading. She put her head down and charged forward, clutching her purse tightly to her side as if she were boarding a midtown subway during rush hour.

She would have made it inside without having to speak to anyone, except three students holding posters

7

and rolls of tape stopped abruptly in front of the door that was her target, blocking her way. The flow of bodies pressing forward from behind her pushed Karen into the middle of the group.

"Oh, sorry," she mumbled, flustered, trying desperately to back up but hitting a solid wall of humanity.

A girl with soulful, dark eyes turned and observed Karen. She didn't exactly smile, but the twist of her lips expressed her pleasure at seeing her. "No problem. We're undoubtedly doing this at the wrong time of day." She held up a large cardboard sign that was brightly smeared with colored marker and glitter. "I was about to tape this to the door. We've put up the others along the halls, but this is the best place to attract everyone's attention."

Karen sensed the two boys who flanked the girl studying her intently, and an anxious shiver rippled down her spine. *They're checking out my fat stomach. Oh, God!*

"Here." The girl thrust a roll of transparent tape at her. "I'll hold it up. You stick on the tape."

Karen longed to duck beneath the sea of students surging around her. However, she was obviously expected to lend a hand. She pulled off a long piece of tape and smacked it down across one corner of the poster, then smoothed the ends over the cold metal door. Shivering in the icy wind, she repeated the process at each of the remaining corners.

"That's great. Thanks so much." The girl faced her and, finally, smiled. "I'm Nona Stewart."

"Karen Henderson." She smiled in return.

"Is this your first day at Killington?"

"Yes," Karen admitted regretfully. She'd just been thinking that Nona's broad-sounding but pleasant voice was very different from those of her old friends.

Something about her own speech must have marked her as an out-of-stater. "We moved to Vermont just before Christmas."

Nona squinted at her, then seemed to read her mind. "You *do* have a little accent, but I like it. You sound very sophisticated." Her glance drifted off thoughtfully toward the parking lot. "Nice car."

"Thanks."

"Welcome to Killington Regional," one of the boys who was standing beside Nona said. "I'm Kurt Haller."

Karen lifted her eyes—daring to look straight at his face for the first time—and was totally blown away. This boy had the most beautiful silver-blond hair she had ever seen—natural she'd be willing to guess—and pale blue eyes that twinkled at her in the frosty morning air. He was tall and slender and reminded her of a Viking prince. But there was something else unusual about him. She wrinkled her nose in concentration, trying to place it.

Kurt laughed. "You're thinking I have the most accent of all? Right?"

"Right." She smiled, for now that he mentioned it, his voice did have a musical, foreign ring—sort of like Arnold Schwarzenegger's. However, Kurt's accent tended to slip away at times, like that of an actor who hasn't quite mastered his character. For a moment she just stared at him, fascinated, then the other boy stepped in front of Kurt.

"The name's Matt, Matt Welch," he said solemnly, holding out his hand. He was short, not much taller than her own 5'6", but the strength in his handshake revealed he was in great physical condition. "Welcome to Killington, Karen. As it happens, this is your lucky day. You've bumped into the most influential people in this school."

"Matt, quit it." Nona nudged him with mild reproof. "What's gotten into you?" She turned to Karen apologetically. "He's usually the quietest of the three."

"The three?" Karen asked.

"Hey, I can't help if it's true." Matt winked at Karen, brushing sandy curls, too long to be fashionable at her old school, away from his forehead. "They call us the rat pack—Kurt, Brandon, and me."

"Brandon's my brother," Nona said quietly but with a ring of pride in her voice. "He graduated a few years ago and works in one of the clubs on the Access Road."

"Access Road?" Karen felt as if she'd entered a new universe. Now she understood how tourists in New York City felt.

"The street leading up to Snowshed, the central ski slope at Killington Resort," offered Matt. "If you haven't driven it already, you will because you'll be spending half your life there. The Access Road is wall-to-wall nightclubs, take-out restaurants, and ski shops."

Karen was about to admit that she didn't ski, had *never* skied, and probably would kill herself if she tried—when the bell rang. "Oh, I'd better get going," she murmured.

"What classes are you taking?" Matt asked, swinging quickly into step beside her.

Karen fished a computer printout from her purse and handed it to him. Nona and Kurt followed them through the door.

"You have biology in room 112 first period. That's right next door to my chem class," Matt remarked.

"Come on, I'll walk you so you don't get lost."

Karen smiled, sneaking a downward peek, and sucked in her gut. *Good*, she thought, *the sweater didn't budge*. He probably couldn't tell she weighed a ton.

She glanced speculatively over her shoulder at Kurt. Matt was nice, as well as handsome in a comfortable way, but Kurt was exotic, exciting. It might be worth going on a starvation diet with major hunks like this around.

"Is your first class anywhere nearby?" she asked Kurt.

He gave Matt a wintry look, then shrugged. "Not really. I'll see you later, Karen."

With a sinking sensation, Karen watched Kurt disappear down a hallway. But she didn't have time to brood, for Matt was tugging on her arm to hurry her along, and they were soon lost in the press of bodies squeezing through the locker-lined corridors.

At last they reached her classroom. "If you can't find your way around, just stop somebody and tell them you're Matt Welch's friend. They won't steer you wrong."

"Thanks," she said, smiling.

"Everyone eats lunch from noon to twelve-thirty, since the whole school is small enough to fit in the cafeteria at the same time. Join us at our table if you don't already have somewhere else to sit." Matt's soft brown eyes were questioning. He was asking if she already had a boyfriend.

"No. I don't have a place yet." She glanced demurely at him out of the corners of her eyes.

He grinned. "Well, you do now. Nona's sort of like queen bee at Killington. She looks out for everyone, and I could tell she liked you from the moment

11

she spotted you in the parking lot. She always arrives first at the cafeteria and holds our table. Look for her if you beat me there.''

''All right.''

Biology was okay, and Karen managed to find her other morning classes without too much trouble. By the time she reached the cafeteria, however, it was mobbed. She wondered if she'd ever find Matt and his friends.

She was still scanning the room when a voice beside her bubbled cheerfully, ''This seat's free. I'm Rosemary Geer. People call me Rosie.''

Karen looked down. A girl with a petite, elfin face and body to match was gazing up at her hopefully through smoky eyes. If Karen had spotted her in town somewhere, she probably would have guessed she was in seventh or eighth grade. She certainly didn't look old enough to be in high school.

''Glad to meet you, Rosie. I'm Karen Henderson. Thanks anyway, I was looking for some friends.''

''Who?''

''Matt Welch, Nona—''

''Nona Stewart and Kurt Haller . . . *their* crowd.'' There was a distinct note of disapproval in the other girl's tone.

Karen scowled at her. ''So what's wrong with them?''

''Nothing,'' Rosie said sweetly. ''Not a damn thing.'' She bit into an apple, hard.

Karen shrugged and continued searching the hot lunch line, determined to ignore Rosie's odd pettiness. She liked Nona, Matt, and Kurt, and it seemed awfully good fortune that she'd run into them her very first morning.

''Look,'' Rosie inserted between chews, ''I

12

shouldn't say anything. I suppose they're not so bad. It's just that they practically run this school, you know. Nona is senior class president this year. Her brother Brandon was president before he graduated.''

"Nona is a class president?" The quiet brunette had seemed an unlikely type to seek public office. Karen decided there must be some hidden strain of grit in Nona not evident on first inspection.

"Yeah. And Matt and Kurt are tied for first place on the popularity scale. Their parties are the best . . . at least that's what I hear—never having been invited to one.'' Rosie looked up inquisitively. "What year are you?"

Karen glanced around again, still watching for her new friends. "I'm a junior."

"Oh."

"You?" she asked, to be polite.

"Sophomore. But," Rosie added brightly, "I'm very mature for my age. I'm dating a college man. He's a freshman at Green Mountain College."

Only in Vermont, Karen thought wryly. Even the colleges sounded as if they'd sprung up out of travel brochures. "Oh, there's Matt," she murmured, suddenly spotting him at the salad bar.

Rosie studied her with a thoughtful expression. "Listen, a word of advice. Be careful, Karen. They're a fast crowd.''

"Fast crowd?" She laughed out loud. "Listen, I can tell you've never been in New York City—you don't know fast until you've walked down Broadway on a Saturday night.''

Rosie's pinched little face seemed to stiffen. "I'm serious. Watch out for yourself. Power is addictive. Nona's buddies think they can run everyone's life, do anything.''

13

Karen gave her an amused smile and started to turn away, but Rosie's hand shot out, stopping her. "Listen to me," she persisted. "When they like you, you're on top of the world. If they dump you—" Rosie opened her free hand, revealing only air "—you're nothing again."

"Well, thanks for the advice," Karen said breezily.

By the time she was halfway across the cafeteria, Karen had totally dismissed the girl. Rosie was probably just ticked off that she hadn't accepted her offer of a seat. Or else she was one of those jealous types, always putting down the in-crowd because she wasn't among them.

Matt saw Karen coming and waved. He led her to a table in a little alcove, away from the rowdier students. Kurt and Nona were already seated there and seemed to be deep in conversation.

"I thought you'd gotten lost," Matt said.

"No, I was just talking to someone."

"Rosie Geer?" Nona said suddenly, surprising her since she hadn't seemed to be paying attention up to this point.

"Yes," Karen admitted hesitantly. "She seems a little . . . odd."

"Odd is putting it mildly. She's a local minister's daughter, which I expect accounts for a lot." Nona poked at the salad in front of her with a plastic fork and eyed Karen speculatively. "She probably had some choice things to say about us."

"Nothing much," Karen lied. She didn't want to be put in the position of an informant.

"She's harmless," Kurt said, giving Nona a meaningful look.

Nona shrugged.

"Do you ski?" Matt asked, changing the subject.

"No," Karen admitted.

"What do you do for fun?" Nona asked.

"I shop. I'm a great shopper. I can spot a bargain at forty paces in Bloomies." Karen grinned, remembering all the great times she and her friends had shared—gearing up for school the last week of August, buying Christmas presents, hitting the end-of-season sales. Those days seemed so long ago now. "And I can ice skate," she said eagerly. "I used to skate on the outdoor rink at Rockefeller Center."

"That sounds exciting." Sounding genuinely interested, Matt slid his can of soda in front of her. "I'll bet you're a beautiful skater."

I used to look pretty damn good in one of those skintight skating leotards and teeny-tiny skirts. Instead of answering, Karen just blushed and took a sip of his drink.

"Skaters are usually excellent skiers," Kurt said matter-of-factly. "They cut sharp edges."

She glanced across the table at him. His eyes were directed down at his sandwich. With a pang of regret, she realized he couldn't possibly be as intrigued with her as she was with him.

"Kurt is an instructor," Nona explained. "He teaches advanced downhill skiing and learned to ski in Switzerland when he was just a little guy."

"You've skied in Europe?" Karen asked, impressed.

"I was born there but haven't been back in years," Kurt answered abruptly, his expression suddenly serious.

"Oh."

Karen was aware of a strange, silent tension closing in around the table. Nona took a quick bite of salad and chewed rapidly, her face a shade paler than it had

15

been a moment earlier. Matt glanced thoughtfully from Nona to Kurt.

"If you'd like to learn . . . to ski . . ." Kurt continued haltingly. His frosty blue eyes flickered up to meet Karen's.

For a moment, her heart stopped, she ceased breathing, and Karen could have sworn that the world no longer spun on its axis as it had—uninterrupted—for millions of years.

"No way, man!" Matt reached out, looping his arm possessively around her shoulders. "If she learns from anyone, it'll be me. Besides, you'd scare a beginner to death. Probably take her on a black diamond trail the first day."

"All the trails are marked for beginner, intermediate, or advanced skiers. Black diamonds are the most challenging or dangerous—depending on your point of view," Nona explained. "They're reserved for expert skiers, like Kurt and Matt."

Kurt shot Matt a teasing smile. "At least *I* wouldn't strand her halfway down the mountain."

"Hey!" Matt objected. "That girl was a tourist. I just tried to be a little friendly, and she told me to get lost."

"So you left her on a trail four thousand feet up Killington Peak, and *she* got lost instead. Then I had to go out with the ski patrol to look for her," Kurt persisted.

"You found her, didn't you?"

"Yeah." Kurt grinned. "We found her all right. And if you could have heard the names she called you—"

Nona smiled tolerantly at both boys, obviously enjoying their casual bickering. But there was something about their competitiveness that made Karen uneasy.

The bell rang, ending lunch period. Reluctantly, students began to file out of the cafeteria and wander toward their afternoon classes.

"Doing anything after school?" Matt asked, following Karen out of the cafeteria.

"Homework. Looks like some of my teachers expect me to make up the first half of the year in a week."

"Well, you can't study twenty-four hours a day. What you need is a little R and R between work sessions. How about a ski lesson?"

"Oh, I don't know." Karen shook her head. "I don't have skis, or poles or . . . or anything."

"Just wear something warm and not too bulky. I'll take care of the rest. Where do you live?"

"The old white house up on the hill above Route Four."

"The Grady house. I know it. I'll pick you up right after school."

"That's all right," she said quickly. "I'd rather drive myself this time. I have to get to know the area sooner or later."

"Fine. I'll meet you at the Snowshed base lodge, near the novice slope, three-thirty." And he took off down the hallway.

Stunned, Karen stood where Matt had left her as people rushed past, trying to beat the bell that was undoubtedly going to ring any minute. Never in her wildest dreams had she thought she'd be dating a hick. Well, Matt, Kurt, and Nona weren't really hicks. They were dynamic personalities and *clearly* the school leaders. She was grateful for their friendship.

For a moment she lingered in the corridor, fingering the nickel-sized clear glass bauble that hung from a chain around her neck.

Karen gazed sadly down at it. Her grandmother had

given it to her a week before she'd died. The hollow globe was filled with some kind of liquid, and, floating in it, were opal chips. Usually the bits of gem stone shone a pearly white or bluish green, but at the moment they seemed to glow with a faint pink light.

Karen frowned, trying to remember something Nana Gee had told her about the opals. Her grandmother had received the necklace as a gift from a friend she'd known since they were young girls. The woman had become a travel writer and bought the necklace while on a tour of Australia. The rare opal chips were mined in Queensland and . . .

There was more to the story, but she couldn't recall it now.

When she looked up again, the hall had nearly cleared. On her right was a copy of the poster she'd helped Nona put up outside the school that morning.

MOGUL MADNESS PARTY—
SATURDAY, FEBRUARY 2
8 P.M. till whenever
The Wobbly Barn, Killington Access Road
NO ALCOHOL SERVED

The party was almost a month away. Karen wondered who the mogul was, what made him mad, and why anyone would hold a party in a barn that wobbled! She was sure of only one thing: Matt, Kurt, and Nona would be there. Without knowing why, she knew that she wanted to be, too.

Chapter 2

"Dummy, why didn't you ask for his phone number?" Karen muttered under her breath.

By the time she made it through the rest of her classes she'd accumulated even more work than she had expected, coming in during the middle of the year. She staggered to her car in the student parking lot, her arms aching under the weight of a tower of textbooks. Aside from being short of time, she was having second thoughts about strapping her feet to two boards and pointing her body down an icy mountain.

However, since she had no way of contacting Matt—and it definitely wouldn't be nice to stand him up—she decided she had no choice but to postpone her study schedule for an hour or so.

Since she was going to be home for only a few minutes, she didn't bother pulling her car into the garage, which was a separate structure behind the old house. It had a barn-style wooden door that rolled aside on a rusty iron track. There was no lock on the old door, but her father hadn't seemed concerned when she pointed that out to him. In fact, he'd quoted the low local crime rate with pride, as if car thieves didn't exist this far north.

She ran inside, changed into jeans, a warm jersey, wool sweater, and her best down-filled jacket.

The Access Road was five minutes away and started out at a sharp incline that increased over the next three miles. Twisting and coiling its way upward toward steel-wool clouds, it was lined with modern motels, alpine ski lodges, and fast-food joints advertised by hand-painted wooden signs, which took the place of the garish neon of Manhattan. There also were trendy nightclubs and restaurants with obvious skiing themes—like Powderhounds and The Shred—and tourist-trap souvenir shops advertising Vermont maple syrup, aged cheddar cheese, and Killington T-shirts. Discount ski equipment stores boasted phenomenal bargains, but Karen's shopper's instinct told her she'd most likely find none there.

However, Matt had been right. As blatantly commercial as the strip was, she loved it. There was a special excitement here, a feeling that *this* was the place to go for action! Karen drove on, the road climbing higher, the leaden sky growing closer and closer still, almost as if it were reaching out to take hold of her.

Possibly because her mind was elsewhere, she came around the next curve a little too wide. Gripping the wheel firmly, she pulled back onto her own side of the road in plenty of time, but a car speeding in the other direction was, unfortunately, even further over the line and *on her side*! The driver leaned on his horn. At the last possible moment, and without showing any signs of touching his brake, he swerved to his right.

"You jerk!" Karen screamed, flashing him a New York cabby's middle-fingered greeting.

Trembling with rage and delayed fear from the close

encounter, Karen pulled off onto the gravel shoulder. She spun around in the driver's seat and watched as an ancient station wagon lumbered down the hill like a dying dinosaur. Dying or not, it was moving pretty damn fast. If she'd hit that old tank head-on, her little convertible would have folded like an accordion, with her in it.

A good ten minutes passed before she felt steady enough to continue driving.

Even so, by the time she reached the crowded parking lot at Snowshed base lodge her hands were still shaking on the steering wheel. Karen rolled down her window and breathed in the crisp winter air.

"What's wrong? You look like the survivor of a disaster flick." It was Matt. He leaned through her window.

"Some idiot nearly ran me off the road," she complained indignantly. "He must have been going sixty down that hill!"

"What did he look like?"

"I don't know . . . dark hair . . . about our age, I guess. It happened pretty fast."

"What about the car?"

"It was some sort of older model station wagon. You know, the kind that used to have the real side panels instead of stick-on decals."

Matt nodded. "That's Frank Roselli. His father owns Pizza Attack, one of the take-out restaurants you passed on your way here. He drives like a crazy person when he's making deliveries."

"Well, he could have killed me!"

Matt opened her door. "I'll have a word with him next time I see him," he promised. "Come on, let's find you some skis."

It took nearly half an hour to locate molded plastic

rental boots and skis with bindings that fit her to Matt's satisfaction. At last he seemed to approve. "Keep the boots on, but loosen the clamps so you can walk."

"I feel like a deep-sea diver wearing cement blocks on my feet." Karen shifted her boots awkwardly.

Laughing, Matt shouldered her skis and poles. "Don't worry, you look great. And once you're flying down the mountain, you won't even feel those boots, they'll just become part of you."

"Flying down the mountain?" she repeated dubiously, plodding out of the base lodge after him.

They marched across the slushy novice area where a group of preschoolers were taking a lesson from a shapely female instructor. Karen couldn't take her eyes off of the young woman. Even from this distance, she was gorgeous—the equal of any Ford Agency model. Her skin was a delicate porcelain white, flushed prettily by the wind and sun. Her eyes were a soft lavender, and her long hair shone a glossy black, pulled back by a wide turquoise headband that matched her sexy one-piece ski suit.

"That's Jerrie Tilden," Matt remarked, following the line of her gaze. "She's something, isn't she?"

"Yeah," was all Karen could say, wishing she was ten pounds lighter and half as provocative in her jeans and marshmallow jacket.

"She's Kurt's ex. They broke up a couple weeks ago."

"Really?" she murmured, trying not to sound too interested. "How long had they been going together?"

"Three months. That's a record for Jerrie. She likes to move around."

"She looks as if she's a great teacher," Karen commented. "And the kids seem to be enjoying themselves."

In fact, when one of the pint-sized skiers crashlanded, he'd howl with delight, pick himself up, and start off again with even greater energy at Jerrie's cheerful encouragement.

Karen also spent a good deal of her first hour on skis on her ass. But, as Kurt had suggested, her ice skating experience proved invaluable. Before long, with Matt's guidance, she was able to use the edges of her short learning skis to form a wedge to control her speed on the gentle beginners' slope—most of the time.

"Anytime you want to stop, just sit down," he shouted to her one time when she lost her wedge and began sliding too fast.

She tried it, and it worked just great. The only problem was getting up again, which took her ten minutes.

"Remember, *you* control the mountain, don't let it control you," Matt told her on their next run down the novice slope. "That means you ski whatever speed or direction you feel comfortable with. Forget about the other skiers or how steep the hill looks, you can go as slow and as carefully as you need to. After a few weeks, you'll start looking for challenges, and you'll be ready for them."

"Is that a promise?" she asked skeptically.

He gave her an encouraging wink.

Next he taught her how to turn by crouching slightly and pressing a hand on one knee or the other while leaning into the slope of the hill. Once she'd mastered that much, he tucked the weighted end of the Poma lift rope between her legs, and told her to hang on. She obeyed, and the rope dragged her effortlessly up

23

the hill to a higher spot on the beginner slope. After another hour, Karen was thrilled to find herself zig-zagging at a respectable speed all the way to the bottom.

Matt put his arm around her and squeezed. "Hey, you're doing great! No one would guess you'd never been on skis before today."

"Thanks." She was so proud of herself she could have exploded.

Although she had only planned to stay one hour, it was beginning to get dark, and most of the instructors were dismissing their classes. A rapid motion on the mountainside caught Karen's eye, and she traced it to one of the steeper trails. A young man barreled over the rough terrain, his knees flexing like powerful springs as they absorbed each hollow and bump. His pale white-blond hair tucked beneath ski goggles identified him immediately. Following him were a gaggle of younger boys.

"Kurt must be teaching a really advanced group," she commented.

Matt nodded and stopped to watch his friend's dramatic descent down the mountain. "Yeah. He's getting his students ready for the Mogul Challenge next month. Come on, I'll tell you about it over supper, if you're hungry."

"Are you kidding—I'm starved!"

They parked their skis in a rack outside the base lodge and went inside. Almost immediately Matt spotted someone he knew.

"Brandon!" he shouted across the dining hall. Adding in a quieter voice for her benefit, "That's Nona's brother."

A big-boned young man who appeared to be well over six feet tall gave a wave and started toward them. He had vivid red hair, freckles, and a no-nonsense stride that encouraged others to move out of his way.

"Hey, man, how's it going?" Brandon bellowed, smacking Matt on the back. He checked out Karen. Jerking his head in her direction, he mouthed the word "tourist?"

"Naw," Matt said, taking her hand, "this is Karen Henderson. She just moved to town and started school today. I was giving her a little lesson."

"Bet you were," Brandon teased, leering at her.

"Knock it off," Matt warned, although still smiling.

Brandon turned to Karen. "He gives you a hard time, you just come to me, sweetheart. I'll put him in his place real fast." To make his point he gave Matt a playful shove in the shoulder.

Matt shoved him back, but not with any enthusiasm.

"What's up? You two fighting again?" Kurt asked, coming up behind them.

"Hi, ya, killer," Brandon said cheerfully. "Lose any little skiers today?"

"Not a one," Kurt remarked. His accent made it sound like, *nod a vun*. "Although I contemplated leading a couple of the little monsters off a low cliff. They're getting much too cocky for their own good. To appreciate safe skiing, they could use a little taste of fear."

Brandon chuckled. "Just hand 'em over to me for an hour, I'll teach 'em the meaning of fear."

Kurt shook his head. "No thanks, Bran. Their mothers want them back in one piece. Hey, are we eating or what?"

"Brandon and I will get some stuff," Matt volunteered. "Cheeseburgers okay with everyone?"

Karen nodded.

"Sure," said Kurt. "I'll have two . . . no, make that three."

When the other two boys had left to join the cafeteria line, Kurt turned to Karen with a smile. "I saw you out there. You looked good."

"Not as good as Jerrie," Karen said before she could stop herself.

Kurt's eyes clouded.

"I'm sorry, that was stupid. I guess you and she—"

"She and I are nothing," he responded gruffly. "Don't worry about it."

Karen swallowed. Obviously, she'd hit a sensitive nerve. She struggled for a way to switch subjects quickly. "Matt told me that you're a fantastic skier, and he's right. I saw you drilling your students for the Mogul Challenge." She hesitated. "To be honest, I don't know what that is, but it sounds interesting."

Kurt brightened. "The Challenge is a grueling race down a wide, steep trail on Bear Mountain that has been groomed with hundreds of giant moguls—big humps of snow about the size of Volkswagen bugs. The resort erects huge loudspeakers at the bottom of the course and blasts rock music over the whole mountain while the racers try to get to the bottom alive."

"Sounds like fun," Karen said, feeling her pulse speed up just thinking about the treacherous race.

"The competition is tough. Skiers fly in from all over the country. About a quarter of them make it through the qualifying round on the first day. My students usually do pretty well." Kurt sounded proud, and Karen thought he probably had good reason.

"Are *you* racing?" she asked.

26

His eyes sparkled, reminding her of how pure and dazzling a blue they could be when he wasn't brooding as he had been a moment earlier at the mention of Jerrie. "Yeah. Matt, Brandon, and I always race. We generally finish in the top ten. Brandon has won once, I took first place twice, and Matt has come in near the top every year he has entered since he was in seventh grade. He's been training real hard this year. I think he wants to win bad."

"But he ain't got a chance against me!" Brandon bragged with a smug grin as he smacked a tray down on the table between Karen and Kurt.

"The hell I don't!" Matt objected. He slid onto the bench beside Karen. "This is *my* year, guys! You just wait and see. I'll beat both of you by at least five seconds."

"Fat chance!" Brandon laughed.

"Well," said Kurt, looking Matt steadily in the eye, "I guess we'll just have to wait and see who the best man is. Won't we?"

"I guess we will," Matt agreed.

For a long moment the air seemed electric with tension, and Karen felt a shiver of apprehension. Almost without thinking, she touched the necklace at the opening of her jacket. Although she'd just come in from the cold, the glass sphere felt warm against her skin.

It was clear that winning the Challenge meant a great deal to these three boys. She thought it a wonder they'd remained close friends all these years while being such fierce competitors.

But she didn't have long to dwell upon any of this. The boys seemed to forget their argument in the face of food. They dove into the cheeseburgers and fries, and Karen eagerly joined them.

She couldn't remember ever having such a healthy appetite, but she forced herself to stop eating after one burger—even though Matt offered her some of his second one—and a third of the bag of fries she was sharing with him. *If I ski every day and watch what I eat, I'll lose this tummy in no time!* she thought jubilantly.

They were clearing the table of paper cups and wrappers when a short, older man wearing wire-rimmed glasses entered through the doors at the far end of the cafeteria.

Matt elbowed Kurt. "Hey, man, it's your dad."

Kurt swore beneath his breath and turned his back on his father.

Brandon's green eyes darkened, following the older man as he started across the room toward them.

"What's wrong?" Karen whispered to Matt.

Matt laid a finger across his lips to indicate he couldn't explain just then and took her arm, leading her toward the nearest exit. "Come on, Bran," he muttered.

Out of the corner of her eye, Karen could see that Kurt had frozen in the middle of the room, waiting reluctantly as his father approached. Then the heavy glass doors swung shut behind the three of them.

Karen turned to Brandon since Matt still hadn't answered her question. "Kurt and his dad don't get along?" she asked.

"That's an understatement," Brandon bit off. "His old man's a real bastard—"

"Give it a rest," Matt interrupted. "You're always shooting off your mouth about Kurt's dad, and he's no worse than any other father. They just don't get along. Leave it at that."

Brandon glared through the cafeteria window. "Oh,

yeah. If he's so normal, why does Kurt spend four or five nights a week skiing alone in the dark or crashing at my place?''

''Brandon has his own apartment over the garage,'' Matt explained. He turned back to Brandon. ''Look, who knows what goes on between them. It's none of our business, especially since Kurt doesn't want to talk about it. Anyway, Mr. Haller probably just gets ticked off when he doesn't come home at night. My dad would slay me!''

''Yeah, well . . .'' Brandon shot one last dark look through the plate glass. ''If I were Kurt, I wouldn't stand for it. I gotta get to work.'' He swung away from them, then, as if at an afterthought, halted. ''You stopping by tonight? Bring your girl, and I'll get you both in.''

Matt glanced nervously at her. ''I don't know. I have a lot of homework and well . . . you know . . . stuff to do tonight.''

Brandon scowled. ''Likely story, Welch.'' He looked at Karen. ''If Mr. Bookworm here ditches you and you feel like partying tonight, just come by The Drifts. Straight down the Access Road on the right, about a half mile from the base lodge. I'll be at the door.''

Karen smiled unsteadily. ''The Drifts?''

Brandon winked at her and walked away.

''He seems friendly,'' she said. ''Why didn't you want to go?''

''Because he's *stupid*, that's why,'' Matt pronounced. ''Brandon's the bouncer at The Drifts, which is the wildest nightclub on the strip. He could lose his job for letting in underage customers.''

''You've gone before?'' she guessed.

''Oh, yeah, sure.''

"So why not tonight? I've been to plenty of clubs in the city. It's no big deal."

"This isn't New York. Up here it could be a big deal if you get caught." He put an arm around her. "I just don't want to see you get hurt."

Karen looked up into his rich brown eyes. He was trying to protect her. How sweet!

That night, she took Romeo out of his cage and sat down on her bed. The little blue-feathered parakeet perched on her shoulder while she munched potato chips—just a few so she wouldn't ruin her recently begun diet. He happily licked the salt off her fingertips, chirped in her ear, and pecked at the heavy chain around her neck.

"Knock it off," she giggled, holding up her hand so he could hop onto it.

His tiny, cool claws wrapped around her index finger, and she brought her nose down to meet his beak. He kissed her a birdy kiss—all beak and little purple tongue.

"This has been a fantastic day," she confessed. "I started school, hung out with the right crowd, took a skiing lesson with one of the most popular boys in town, and ate supper with three top-notch hunks. Life is definitely looking up."

Chirp, said Romeo.

"Right. Chirp." Karen frowned, looking down at Nana Gee's opals, which were glowing a dull, mysterious pink. For some reason, the odd hue reminded her of blood diluted in water, and the thought made her uneasy. "So," she continued, "why do I feel as if everything's too good to be true? Why do I feel as if something horrible is about to happen?"

Chirp, chirp.

"You're right. Why question a good thing? Just go with the flow!" Karen laid back on her bed, grinning at the ceiling, while Romeo jumped down onto her stomach and started running in circles, his sharp little claws tickling her.

For some reason, it was then that she remembered the rest of her grandmother's story. Karen had gone to visit her in the hospital, and, despite her resolve not to cry, she had burst into tears when her grandmother hugged her, saying the doctors had told her that the cancer had spread and it wouldn't be long to the end.

"You're not crying for me, are you?" Nana Gee had asked.

"Of course I am. Who else would I be crying for?" Karen demanded, sniffling.

"Yourself. Because you are afraid of the future."

Karen opened her mouth to deny it, then considered her grandmother's words. "I suppose I am," she admitted. "The idea of something unexpected happening scares me. I mean, I'd rather know if I only had a year to live . . . so I could do a few of the things I've always wanted."

"I suppose I've always felt the same." Nana coughed and waved at a glass of water on the table beside her bed.

Karen reached over for it and helped her drink. "You knew you were really sick before the doctors had the test results, didn't you?" Karen whispered.

Her grandmother nodded.

"Were you in a lot of pain?"

"No."

Karen was puzzled. "Then how did you know?"

"I was warned . . . in another way." There was a brief, brilliant sparkle in her grandmother's otherwise lusterless hazel eyes. She reached in back of her neck and unclasped the pretty necklace Karen remembered her wearing almost all the time. She placed it in her granddaughter's palm, then closed her own over it. "My dearest friend gave this to me years ago when she was researching an article on Australia, and now I want you to have it. It will always warn you of danger."

Sure that the disease had suddenly affected her grandmother's brain, Karen struggled to keep a straight face. "Danger?"

"Certainly. If you know that you have no real reason to be afraid, then you can let life come to you as it will. You can accept changes that are good and, maybe, avoid circumstances that are evil."

Karen stared skeptically at the gold chain with its attached glass ball.

Her grandmother continued. "The aborigines believe that when opals kept close to the body are white or glow a soft greenish blue, their owner can be sure she is safe and that no one means her any harm. It's only when they begin to turn red that she must question people's motives or fear for her future."

Sometimes Karen wished her grandmother would be a little less dramatic, especially on her deathbed where her strange warning just sounded silly.

But now, six months later, Karen felt a shiver of apprehension slither along her spine as she stared down at the pale pink stones. Was she ill without realizing it? Or did someone mean to harm her? If so, who? She had no enemies.

Karen stared at the stones, wondering if there was some simple scientific explanation for their change in color—the heat of her body, or a fluctuation in barometric pressure. But no matter how she rationalized their mysterious behavior, nothing soothed her jumpy nerves or made it any easier to sleep.

Chapter 3

"Hi, ya!" a squeaky voice hit her from behind.

Karen turned away from her open locker with a grimace. "Hi, Rosie."

It was her second week of school at Killington, and she was fitting right in. Nona had introduced her to a lot of other girls in the junior and senior classes and invited her to join the SGA, Student Government Association, as an intern. Matt had taken her skiing nearly every day, and she was improving rapidly, along with—to her delight—dropping a few more pounds.

In fact, Rosie continued to be the only fly in the Killington ointment. The sophomore seemed to pop up everywhere during the day—between periods, in the cafeteria, at the guidance office during Karen's appointment with her counselor. Karen suspected that Rosie actually followed her around, waiting for Nona and the others to leave.

"I'll walk with you to your next class," Rosie offered this morning.

"Matt's meeting me in front of the science wing," Karen said quickly, hoping she would take a hint and leave her alone. "I'm in a hurry. Sorry."

"Oh." Rosie looked desolate, her smoky eyes glittering softly. She smoothed down the front of her red sweater, which looked hand-knit, and let out a disappointed sigh.

"Oh, come on," Karen groaned. "Walk with me that far."

Rosie beamed.

The halls were far too noisy to hear normal conversation, but Rosie didn't seem to mind as she babbled cheerily about her college boyfriend.

"Does he drive down to see you very often?" Karen shouted above the roar.

Rosie's frown returned. "Not very. He's so busy— all his classes, you know. But I go up to see him whenever I can."

"How? Does your mother or father drive you?"

Rosie gasped, horrified. "Are you kidding? They'd *kill* me if they found out I was dating a college man!"

Karen hid a grin. Obviously, Rosie thought that seeing someone older was a great status symbol. "So, how do you two get together?"

"We talk on the phone and write," Rosie said defensively. "And sometimes," she added, speaking directly into Karen's ear so that no one nearby would hear, "I borrow a car and drive myself."

Karen lifted an eyebrow. "But you don't have a license."

"So? The important thing is I'm a great driver."

"What if you get stopped by a cop?"

"That won't happen," Rosie stated flatly.

Karen laughed. "How do you know?"

"It just won't. Look I gotta go, there's Matt waiting for you. I just wanted to say 'hi' and all that,

36

and . . . oh yeah, one other thing—isn't your dad a doctor?''

Karen squinted at Rosie, wishing she could read the other girl's unpredictable thoughts. "Yeah," she admitted slowly, "he's a doctor. Why?"

"No reason. I just think that's nice. Killington needs good medical professionals. Bye, see ya."

She stood for a moment, watching Rosie dodge off between bodies along the crowded corridor, looking like an out-of-control bumper car at an amusement park. "Now what was that all about?" she muttered. Turning with a shrug, she expected to find Matt.

He wasn't there.

Confused, Karen searched up and down the hallway, but was still unable to find him. *Weird*, she thought. Hadn't Rosie just seen him?

The bell marking the beginning of the next period rang, and the halls cleared as if by magic. The rules at Killington were strict. No one was allowed in the halls without a pass between classes. If you were caught, it meant an automatic after-school detention— no exceptions.

Karen hurried toward her classroom, sorry that she'd missed Matt, but unwilling to lose time with him after school for being apprehended by a teacher. She had nearly reached the door when she heard angry voices coming from somewhere close by. Curiosity getting the better of her, she paused, listening.

"You can't do that! You'll get caught!" The voice was husky but still might have been either a girl's or a boy's.

"We won't get caught if we handle it right," retorted a second person.

"Right? You're talking about murder, for God's sake!"

Karen's heart jumped into her throat. Murder? She looked up and down the hallway. No one was in sight. Stepping up to the nearest door, a janitor's closet, she placed her ear against the surface. Nothing.

Her heart pounded in her chest and her mouth felt dry. Without contemplating what she'd do if the speakers caught her in the act of spying on them, she moved silently to the next door and held her breath as she listened again.

"Hey, keep it down," the second voice warned. "You want the world to know? Look, even if you're not with me on this, I'm going ahead."

"You know I'm with you. How can I not be?"

"Fine. We've got all the proof we need—there's no question now. We'll kill the bastard first chance we get."

Karen swallowed over the lump in her throat. Her hands trembling, she backed quickly away from the door. Slowly, her eyes rose to the black, stenciled letters over the door.

DRAMA DEPT.—MS. JESSUP

With a groan of relief Karen shook her head and smiled dimly. Murder. Of course, she reassured herself, they must just be rehearsing lines.

However, as she hurried off to her class, a strange feeling of foreboding followed her. Absentmindedly, she pulled the gold chain out of the neckline of her sweater, cupping the delicate, clear glass globe in her palm so that it wouldn't thump against her chest as she ran.

Just before she pulled open the classroom door, she glanced down and noticed that the crystals, which had

38

been blue again that morning when she woke up, were once more a diluted bloody pink.

February

The Saturday morning of the qualifying round of the Mogul Challenge was overcast. Standing at the top of the snow-covered Outer Limits Trail on Bear Mountain, the icy February wind burning his cheeks, Kurt looked up at the gray sky and was pleased. A couple more inches of fresh, natural snow could only make the course better. If you hit an icy patch and fell on this slope, chances were you wouldn't stop sliding until something substantial—like a tree or boulder—stopped you.

Rock music blared from a half dozen huge speakers set up outside the base lodge. Scattered behind the glass and natural wood building were picnic tables that had been cleared of snow that morning, along with several industrial-size charcoal grills. Many in the audience at the foot of the mountain were also participants. They wore paper numbers pinned to their jacket backs and joked with friends as they watched the last practice runs. All in all, the event encouraged a carnival atmosphere. Everyone was ready for a good time.

Kurt, on the other hand, always took his skiing seriously. He eyed the trail below, which from this angle looked almost like a straight drop. *I'm going to win this year . . . no matter what*, he thought with determination.

Two figures skied up behind him and stopped.

"Looks like a good turnout," Matt observed cheerfully. "Still twenty minutes before the preliminary timed runs start, and there must be six or seven hundred people down there."

39

"Tomorrow will be mobbed," Kurt murmured, automatically searching the crowd for one special spectator.

"Karen should be here soon," Matt said casually.

Kurt jumped, uneasy at the thought that Matt might have guessed he was looking for her. But then, how could Matt have known his best friend was crazy about his girl? Kurt had been very careful to steer clear of Karen at school as well as on the slopes when she was practicing alone. Matt had made it clear from the start that he was interested in the pretty blond New Yorker, and out of respect for their friendship, Kurt had grudgingly stepped aside.

Now, a month later, he was beginning to wonder if that had been such a great idea. Vermont seemed to agree with Karen. She'd slimmed down, and her cheeks were always prettily flushed when he ran into her and they exchanged a word or a nod. His attraction to her was growing, instead of fading as he'd expected it would.

"There are the girls!" Brandon announced, pointing with his ski pole.

Almost immediately, Kurt spotted Nona in her pale blue ski suit. Karen stood beside her in her new one-piece outfit, a golden yellow that stood out against the snow like gleeful sunlight and matched her long hair, blowing loose and silky in the wind. God, how he'd love to touch her!

"Come on, guys. Let's show 'em how it's done!" Matt called from the starting gate. He lowered his goggles into place over his eyes, gripped his poles, and pushed off.

Brandon quickly followed with Kurt a close third. He studied Matt's and Brandon's style from behind as they wove down the slope. Matt was normally a cautious skier, although today he was pushing himself to his limit, taking risks to stay ahead of his friends. Brandon, on the other hand, was always a wild man. The athletic redhead plummeted down the mountainside without any apparent fear for his life, snow sizzling beneath his skis.

Kurt cut his edges in deep and slalomed through the first shallow valleys between moguls, then flexed his knees to take the wicked jolts over the toughest humps farther down the mountain. For some reason, the knowledge that Karen was down there watching made him take extra chances, too. He dug his poles into the cold white grains, pushing for extra speed.

Karen watched the three boys speeding down the mountainside. They were a breathtaking sight, negotiating the dangerous hollows and hills with seemingly effortless grace.

In fact, it looked as if an architect in league with the devil himself had been commissioned to design the Outer Limits. Small humps in the snow still challenged Karen's balance and agility. But these gigantic moguls were a shock to the knees and made successful completion of the run almost impossible for all but the most advanced skiers. The mountainside looked more like a crater-strewn moonscape than a normal ski trail.

As she watched, Karen became familiar with the rules. The contestants had to ski from the top, zigzagging over moguls while performing as many daring stunts as possible *and* clocking the best possible time to the bottom. This was hotdog skiing at its best.

"Oh, no!" Nona sucked in her breath and grabbed

Karen's arm as Brandon caught a tip of one ski and seemed about to crash.

"It's all right," Karen reassured her a second later. "He's got his balance again. Look."

Nona shook her head with sisterly concern. "He takes too many chances."

"They're all very aggressive skiers," Karen observed. Out of loyalty she was mostly watching Matt, praying he'd complete his practice run without mishap. But her eyes kept wandering higher up the treacherous slope to Kurt. His grace and speed were mesmerizing. His pale hair whipped out behind his head, then suddenly he launched himself into a perfect flip with a half twist that set the crowd to cheering and clapping.

"What a show-off," Nona said fondly. "The boys usually save that sort of stuff for the real thing."

"Kurt is a bit of a ham," Karen admitted, blushing. Had he known she was here? But, no, he was probably just playing to the audience.

A minute later, all three boys had joined them.

"How'd we look?" Matt asked, gasping for air.

"Fantastic," Karen assured him.

He took her hand and squeezed it. "Wait till you see my qualifying run."

Brandon chuckled. "Yeah. It'll be only about ten seconds slower than mine!"

"You wish!" Matt exclaimed, punching Brandon good-naturedly in the arm.

"Sorry, guys, the mountain's mine this year," Kurt announced in a quiet but determined tone.

They all turned to stare at him, and Karen was struck by the cold assurance in his frosty blue eyes. It made her wonder if he always got what he wanted and what price he'd be willing to pay.

"Says who?" Brandon demanded, an angry edge to his words.

Kurt shrugged. "Sometimes you want something and can't have it. You just have to accept the way things are." He glanced meaningfully at Karen, and she felt her heart flutter. Then he turned back to Brandon. "Other times, you don't give up so easy." His accent seemed to thicken. "The Bear is mine this year!"

With that he V-kicked his skis, turning his back on them, and skied away.

"Well, what got into him?" Matt asked, his arm draped over Karen's shoulder.

She frowned, watching Kurt disappear behind the restaurant end of the base lodge. The grills were already smoking fragrantly with barbecued chicken, plump sausages, hot dogs, and hamburgers. "I don't know," she murmured.

"Well, if you ask me," Nona said, "I think you all take this race much too seriously. Why can't you be more like . . . like . . ." She looked around for an example and grabbed a passing shoulder. ". . . more like Frank here."

Two boxed pizzas balanced above his head on one hand, Frank Roselli swerved to a precarious stop in the slippery snow. His tennis shoes appeared to be soaked through. "Hey, cool it, Nona. I got a delivery to make."

"You always got a delivery to make, Frank," Nona teased. "That's why I love you. Life is so simple for you."

Frank blushed. "Thanks . . . I think," he stammered. Then flashing her a shy smile, he slipped out of her grip and disappeared into the mob.

Karen smiled. "I think he likes you."

Nona tipped her head to one side. "I thought he did for a long time. But he's never asked me out."

"He seems bashful."

Nona laughed. "We've known each other since seventh grade. How bashful can he be?"

"You can do better than him," Brandon grumbled, unimpressed.

"He's nice," Nona defended Frank.

"Why don't *you* ask *him* out?" Karen suggested. "It's the nineties, you know."

Nona seemed to consider that. "Maybe I will. I'll see how things—"

Brandon abruptly seized her arm. "Hey, let's have something to eat before the time trials start. You want a beer with yours?"

Nona looked up at him with wide eyes that, at first, seemed concerned but quickly cleared. "Sounds like a good idea. But I'm tired, I want to sit down. Get me a hot dog, please. With mustard and relish."

Brandon observed her for a moment. "You sure you don't want to come with me to fix it yourself?"

Nona waved him off. "No. Any way you fix it is fine with me . . . really."

For a second, the brother and sister looked at each other as if sending subtle messages back and forth, and Karen sensed a lessening tension between them. Brandon straightened up and went to join the food line.

"You hungry?" Matt asked Karen.

"A little," she admitted.

"I'll get you a burger," he said quickly, knowing she preferred them to hot dogs.

"What's wrong with Brandon?" Karen asked when the boys had left.

Nona shook her head. "I suppose he's just nervous . . . about the race."

"Are you sure that's all?"

"Sure," Nona said, watching her brother as he stood patiently in line. "What else could it be?"

As the first skier started down the mountain for the timed runs, the rock music tripled in volume. The song was "Wipe Out" and, as though jinxed by the music, poor number one crashed on the third mogul and slid the rest of the way down the steep slope before coming to an embarrassing stop at the feet of several spectators. To Karen's surprise, the second skier was Jerrie Tilden, and she did much better, making it three-quarters of the way down the deeply pitted course before falling when she attempted a split leap.

"She was good!" Karen gasped, clapping enthusiastically as Jerrie picked herself up and brushed off, apparently unhurt.

"Not as good as Brandon," Nona proclaimed proudly, looking up at the chair lift.

Karen could see Matt's tan ski jacket and his skis dangling from his feet. On one side of him was Brandon in bright red, all pent-up energy, kicking at the iron foot rest. On the other was Kurt, in black, gazing moodily at the slope below.

Nona's eyes glowed with adoration for her brother as he stepped up to the starting gate a couple of minutes later. When the starter gave the signal, Brandon crouched and gave himself a fierce push with his ski poles. He flew down the course, launching himself high into the air over moguls, dipping low between them, using his knees to cushion the shock of each landing, and throwing in a daredevil flip now and then.

By the time he reached the bottom of the mountain, the crowd was screaming with delight.

A skier from Colorado followed. He successfully completed the course, but his time was much slower than Brandon's, and he didn't put on nearly as exciting a show.

Matt was next.

Karen crossed every finger on both hands and held her breath. She could feel her heart pounding as he crouched beside the starter, poles tucked between his arms and ribs. Although she was too far away to make out his expression, she could tell by his rigid stance that he was tense. His competitiveness was evidently every bit as strong as Brandon's and Kurt's.

The starter lifted one hand as a signal. Matt was off.

"Oh!" Karen squealed a few seconds later. "He's doing great. Did you see that jump he just made?"

"His time is slow," Nona said, her voice uncharacteristically taut and chilled.

Karen stared at her. "This is just the trials."

Nona didn't answer but continued to stare at Matt as he descended the mountain.

Matt nearly lost his balance on the last mogul, but he recovered in time to slide through the finish gate, poles held triumphantly high. Karen ran to him and gave him a big hug. He was breathing raggedly, his cheeks pink as he pulled his goggles up onto his forehead and squeezed her back.

"How'd I look?" he gasped.

"Like a champ," Karen said, grinning.

Still breathing hard, Matt waited for his time as Brandon walked over.

"One-forty-four!" the announcer called out.

"Tough luck old man," Brandon said smugly, "got you again."

Matt gave him a deadly look. "So what? We both qualify. Tomorrow's the finals."

"You'll never do it," Brandon taunted, wagging a finger at him.

"Watch me," Matt growled.

Nona stood by, looking nervous but wisely staying out of the argument.

"Hey," Karen interrupted with an uneasy laugh, unable to tell if they were playing or serious, "lighten up. You guys are best friends. Remember?"

"Friendship only takes you so far," Matt mumbled, looking away.

Karen noticed that Kurt was poised at the top of the run. When his name was announced, a roar went up from the crowd. That was enough to catch Matt's and Brandon's attention and cool the static vibrating between them.

"Kurt must be a favorite," Karen remarked.

Matt chuckled. "Kurt has a bunch of lady groupies that follow him around all weekend—lucky dog."

"Hey!" Karen jabbed him reproachfully with an elbow. "You've got me."

"Yeah," he said, smiling at her softly. "I've got you, and Kurt doesn't." Something of his earlier macho tone remained and caught her attention.

"What does that mean?" Karen asked.

"Nothing."

"It does. You sounded as if *I* were a race, too."

Matt shrugged. "In a way, you were. But that doesn't matter anymore."

Kurt had started down the mountain, but Karen wasn't paying much attention. "Tell me," she insisted.

Matt shook his head, irritated. "Look, don't get all bent out of shape. Just . . . the first day you arrived at school in that hot car with New York plates . . . well, we all noticed you right away. Nona made some comment about you being the new girl in town. She works as an aide in the administration office fourth period, and she'd heard a new student was coming. So she was wondering out loud what lucky guy was going to land you. She said something about Kurt and me not standing a chance."

Karen grimaced. Nona should have known better. Dropping something like that within hearing of those two boys was like waving a red flag in front of a pair of bulls. The only question would be, which one would charge first?

"You mean, the two of you were competing for me?"

Matt winced. "Well, sort of . . . not for long. I mean, Kurt gave up the fight pretty early on."

"Why?"

"Huh?"

Karen knew her question sounded ridiculous, but suddenly the answer was important to her. "Why didn't Kurt fight for me? Not literally, of course—you know what I mean."

"I told him you were mine, to bug off."

Karen stared at Matt in disbelief, but he turned around to watch Kurt. She looked up in time to see his shiny black ski suit weaving almost effortlessly down the steep slope, veering over moguls, dipping gracefully and, now and then, lifting in a dramatic leap or midair helicopter spin. She could imagine his blue eyes—sharp, concentrating on each move, calculating the placement of his skis for the best traction and control. He seemed to be descending in slow motion, and yet the snow was spraying from beneath the edges of his skis, so she knew he must be traveling very fast.

When the announcer gave Kurt's time, the crowd went wild. He was just three seconds off Brandon's pace.

So, she thought, *Kurt is a gentleman. He stepped aside for his friend.* And suddenly Karen wasn't sure how she felt about being competed for, as if she were the prize in a tournament, then dropped—even if it was due to loyalty to an old friend.

Although her heart wasn't in it, she forced herself to walk over to the finish gate along with the others. Nona gave Kurt a hug, and Matt and Brandon, playing the good sports, patted him on the back. There was a lump in her throat as she stepped forward and murmured, "Congratulations, Kurt. You were super."

He looked at her for a second too long—or was that her imagination?—then averted his glance. "Thanks."

Matt grumbled. "I had to take it a little slow. My ankle was bothering me."

"Sure," Brandon teased. "Got any more excuses?"

"It's not an excuse!" Matt insisted. "I hurt it on the practice run."

"That's news to me." Brandon laughed, winking at Kurt, who didn't seem amused. "Come on, men. Let's hit the showers."

"We'll meet you out here," Nona said. She rubbed her forehead and winced as the boys took off for the locker room.

"Those three could give anyone a headache," Karen commented wryly.

Nona sighed. "It's not them. I've had it since last

night. I didn't sleep at all, and now I can hardly see straight it hurts so much."

"Well, you can stop worrying about Brandon. He made the cut without breaking his neck," Karen said encouragingly.

Nona buried her face in her hands. "I wasn't thinking about today."

Of course, tomorrow would be even more grueling, with increased pressure on all the racers. "Why don't you sit down. I'll go and get you a Coke," Karen offered. "Maybe the caffeine will help."

"Thanks. Thanks a lot," Nona whispered thickly.

Karen walked across the slushy observation area toward the line of people at the outside bar. Halfway there, she was intercepted by Rosie Geer.

"Hi!" the younger girl said brightly.

"Hi, Rosie, what's up?" Karen didn't stop to chat but continued straight for the end of the line so that Nona wouldn't have to wait through a long conversation for her soda.

"Nothing much," Rosie said, falling into step beside her. "What are you getting?"

"A soda, for Nona."

"Is she too special to buy her own drinks now?" Rosie asked sarcastically.

"She has a headache, all right?" Karen knew she sounded marginally bitchy, but she had lost her patience with Rosie. The girl had a real attitude problem.

"Oh, a headache," Rosie mused. "So you're doing her a favor? That's nice."

"I think so."

"Listen. Since you're in the mood for doing favors, I wonder if you might do just one more. A little one for a friend, like for me."

Something in Rosie's tone set off a warning alarm

in Karen's brain. "It depends what the favor is," she said warily.

"Nothing much." Nevertheless, Rosie lowered her voice. "See, I sort of ran out of my pills, and I thought since your father is a gynecologist, well, he must have oodles of samples lying around, and—"

Karen swung around and glared at Rosie. "You're asking me to steal drugs from my father for you?"

"Not *steal* really, just sort of borrow." Rosie blinked at her sheepishly. "After all, he must get them for free, so what will it cost you?"

"My *life*, if he catches me!" Karen retorted grimly.

"Oh, come off it—"

"I'm serious. If you're on the Pill, call your doctor for a refill."

"That's it? You won't help me?" Rosie asked in disbelief.

Karen looked into her innocent little-girl eyes. Were they really that young and naive? Or was Rosie trying to manipulate her?

"What's the name of the drug in your prescription?" Karen asked.

"The name?" Rosie rolled her eyes, as if trying to recall it. "Aren't they all the same? I mean, the Pill is just the Pill. Right?"

"No. There are dozens of types, strengths, and dosage plans. It's important that you take the one that's right for you." Karen, in fact, had been taking Norlestrin for several years for the wicked cramps that had kept her home from school the first two days of every period.

Rosie looked deflated. "I forget the name," she mumbled.

"You don't have a prescription, do you?"

"I . . . well, I—"

51

"Do you?"

"No," Rosie admitted in a whisper, "but I would if I could. It's my parents. Since my dad is a minister, he knows every physician in town. They must hold conventions of doctors and ministers in hospitals, I don't know. Anyway, I can't make an appointment to have an ingrown toenail treated without my parents getting a call. There's no privacy around a small town like this."

"So, why do you need the Pill? Is your boyfriend pressuring you to have sex?"

Rosie laughed. "Not exactly." The line moved up, and she took two steps forward to stay close to Karen. "First Chuck said he wouldn't because I was too young. Finally he admitted that he was afraid I'd get pregnant—because he'd heard of accidents happening, even with condoms. So I said I'd go on the Pill, and he said okay, let him know as soon as I started."

Karen smiled to herself. Whoever this guy was, he sounded a good deal more sensible about sex than Rosie. She seemed too immature for a serious relationship. He must have realized that and known, as well, that she'd have a tough time getting hold of birth control pills.

Karen patted Rosie's arm. "I'm sorry. I can't help you."

The sophomore stared at her in shock, then yanked her arm away angrily.

"Look, it's dangerous taking medication without a doctor examining you," Karen tried to explain. "Besides, I could never steal from my own father, and if I did, he'd figure out it was me."

Tears sprang to Rosie's eyes. "You're just like Nona and her crowd. Selfish! You have a boyfriend and popular people to hang out with, and you think

52

you're part of their stupid little group. But you're wrong!'' Rosie's voice quivered with emotion. "They're using you. You're so enchanted by them you can't see it, but they're the devil's soldiers!''

"May I help you?" a young man asked from behind the food counter as Rosie bolted off through the crowd.

"Huh?" Karen shook herself free of watching the sophomore's retreating figure. "Oh, yeah . . . two Cokes, please. Hold the pills . . . I mean, the ice."

Chapter 4

Someone handed the cop two paper cups of black coffee. "Here," he said, extending one toward Karen.

She took it gratefully with chilly fingertips. Would she ever feel warm again? Why was it that you didn't realize how close you had become to a person until it was too late? It had been that way with her grandmother, and, in the moments following the accident, she felt almost at one with this person she'd met only a month before. She felt as if her own bones had been crushed, her skull splintered, her existence banished to a bleak, friendless eternity.

"Drink some coffee," the officer advised.

She did, then peeked over the lip of the cup at his badge, her head feeling a fraction clearer. Mancini, it said. Like the composer. She tried to hum the "Pink Panther" theme in her head, imagining the impish cartoon character, hoping it would make her smile. It didn't.

"I know this is difficult, but concentrate very hard on every detail now," he cautioned her. "The part that happened next is most important—the party."

"Yes," she murmured, then took another sip of the steaming black liquid for strength.

When she looked up, she realized for the first time that she and Officer Mancini were alone in the party room. The other kids must have been dismissed to go home. How she wished she'd been with them! She longed for her room, for her own soft bed and Romeo and home-baked cookies and cold milk and—yes— even for her parents. She wondered where her mother and father were now, and if they'd even been notified that she was being questioned by the police.

"Go on, Karen—everything, no matter how insignificant you may think it is."

With a tired nod, she continued.

It was close to five o'clock when the telephone rang. Karen was just stepping out of the shower. She had her own line because of her father's profession, and no one else ever answered her phone. Trailing water after her, she padded across her bedroom in a towel, squealing as the cold air hit her wet skin.

"Hello?" she answered, shivering.

"Hi, it's Nona. You all ready?"

"Well, almost . . . a few clothes, dry hair, and some makeup will help. I've got plenty of time. The party doesn't start until eight."

Nona groaned. "Maybe this isn't such a good idea."

"What isn't such a good idea?" Karen asked, wishing Nona would come to the point. She was growing egg-sized goose bumps.

"I was going to ask if I could pick you up in fifteen minutes so you could help me decorate before the party—but I guess I can do it myself."

"What about the rest of the decoration committee?

Weren't you all supposed to be finished by now?" Karen asked.

Nona let out a long, exasperated sigh. "Sharon Field sprained her ankle in the qualifying run. Merry Jacobson begged off at the last minute to visit her boyfriend in Springfield. And Tanya Krest is a jerk and wants to ruin everything by stapling lewd rock posters to the walls, so I told her not to bother coming."

Karen rethought her preparations for the evening. If she blew-dry her hair instead of setting it and wore her red blouse (which was already hanging in her closet) instead of the blue one (which needed ironing) and skipped polishing her nails—

"You go on ahead to the Wobbly. I'll meet you there as soon as I can," she promised.

Nona made a dissatisfied sound in the receiver. "Look, I'm a little nervous about tonight," she admitted. "I want everything to look perfect since I'm responsible for the decorations. What if you get held up, or your car won't start or something?"

"You worry too much."

"Let me pick you up in half an hour. Is that enough time?" Nona persisted.

"Fine," Karen agreed. "I'll be ready. Just honk when you get here." As soon as she hung up the phone, she dove for the hair dryer.

The nightclub was called the Wobbly Barn because, on nights when the music was loudest and the dancers most energetic, the walls—which had been erected from the weathered remains of ten old barns—were said to shake or wobble by as much as six degrees.

The snow had started falling heavily around three o'clock that Saturday just after Matt, Brandon, and Kurt had finished their qualifying runs on Bear Mountain. By early that evening when Karen and Nona arrived at the Wobbly Barn, another three inches had been added to the already impressive drifts. By the time they completed their hasty decorations, the snow lay almost a foot thick in the parking lot.

Pink-cheeked skiers burst through the rustic wooden doors, puffing frosty breaths, stomping thick sugary-white crusts off their boots. Sitting at a table in the foyer near the door, Karen rested from her labor, sipping a soda, watching people enter in excited groups.

Matt, Kurt, and Brandon arrived together.

Kurt gave Karen a quick look from under lowered lids while Matt and Brandon hung up their coats. He averted his glance before anyone but Karen noticed it. With a lump in her throat, she watched him turn away and walk into the party room.

"Hey, there's my woman!" Matt called out, taking her hand. He guided her into the room that had been reserved for the Mogul Madness party. "The place looks super!" he shouted above the blaring music, hugging her appreciatively. Tonight the band was playing all sixties oldies in honor of the Wobbly Barn's twenty-fifth anniversary.

She smiled. "It should look good. I spent the last two hours blowing up balloons. I thought my cheeks would pop."

She and Nona had also hung purple-and-gold streamers and a huge papier-mâché figure in the shape of a portly king—the Mogul himself—above the dance floor. In front of a lovely stone fireplace, a long table draped with a crepe paper tablecloth was loaded down with hot and cold finger foods and two enormous punch bowls—both of which had no doubt been spiked by then.

The music softened, and the lights lowered. "You

did great today, yourself,'' Karen whispered into the neck of Matt's shirt as he maneuvered her, still in his embrace, into a slow sway on the dance floor.

For a tender moment Karen rested her head against Matt's shoulder, feeling the music swell in her veins and the warmth of his body envelop her. She nestled closer to him, wishing the song could last forever, but also wishing in her secret heart of hearts that she could dance, just once, with Kurt. If only to see if she felt any different in his arms.

Then she caught Matt watching her expression. ''You're gorgeous,'' he muttered lustily, kissing her on the mouth.

Karen pushed him back gently, thinking she'd caught a telltale whiff that wasn't his usual cologne. ''Beer?''

''Yeah. So?''

''I thought this was supposed to be a dry party?'' Not that she cared, but she was curious. Spiked punch bowls were expected. She tended to stay away from them herself. You never could tell what lethal combination of booze might be lurking in there. And someone always managed to smuggle in a couple of six-packs of beer.

Matt shrugged. ''We had a couple over at Brandon's place. You know, to wind down a little after the trials.''

Sadly, the music faded away, to be replaced by the disc jockey with ''Money, Money'' at a couple thousand decibels. Reluctantly, Karen backed out of Matt's arms.

''Hey, man!'' Brandon swept past, dancing with Jerrie Tilden, who looked more beautiful than ever in the light from the fireplace. They were twirling around the room in a bizarre waltz to the heavy rock beat. On his next pass, he reached into his flannel shirt, pulled out a fresh Coors, and handed it to Matt. "Have one on me!"

"Thanks," Matt shouted above the music as Brandon and his partner disappeared behind a curtain of thrashing bodies.

Karen didn't say anything. If Matt had too much to drink, she'd drive him home in his car, and he could pick it up at her place in the morning.

"Are Brandon and Jerrie seeing a lot of each other?" she asked. Since she'd heard that Kurt and Jerrie had only recently broken up, Karen wondered how it might affect him if Jerrie started dating one of his best friends.

"I don't know," Matt said, sounding bored with the thought. "Jerrie sees a lot of everyone."

A thought struck Karen. "Did you ever date her?"

"Sure. We went together for a while—something like six weeks."

A jealous twinge nibbled at the pit of her stomach. "I didn't realize that. Did you really like her, or was it just because she's so gorgeous?"

Matt shrugged. "Doesn't matter now. It's over. That's the way Jerrie is—some good times, then on to the next man in line."

So, she'd dumped Matt.

"Except with Kurt," Matt continued in a distant voice. "I think she was really hung up on Kurt. He turned the tables on her, though. *He* dropped her."

"Really?"

"Yeah. She trailed him all around the school for days, but he wouldn't have anything to do with her."

Hard to believe, Karen thought wryly. She couldn't imagine any boy turning down a chance to tangle with a body like Jerrie's. She watched the sexy ski instructor

60

break free of her waltz position and perform a little bump-and-grind routine on the dance floor opposite Brandon. In a hot-pink satin jumpsuit, almost as tight as her stretch ski outfit, her awesome breasts and shapely hips were shown off to their best advantage. Not only did she have Brandon's full attention, but she'd secured the salivating interest of most of the male population of the room. In fact, only Kurt, replenishing the pile of logs on the fire, seemed untouched by Jerrie's performance.

Karen looked up at Matt and caught him eyeing the sensual black cascade of Jerrie's hair as if he'd like to dive in.

"Matt!"

"Huh?" His heavy-lidded glance slid back to her, still unabashedly aroused.

"You're with me!" Karen reminded him, kicking herself for sounding so possessive but nevertheless annoyed with him.

"Of course." He gave her a perfunctory kiss on the cheek. "Of course I am." He touched the necklace that rested on her sweater. "That's pretty, and sort of unusual. You wear it a lot."

"It was my grandmother's," she huffed, still angry.

However, Matt seemed unaware of her dark mood. He turned the little globe upside down and watched the crystals float for a moment before settling to the bottom again. "It reminds me of those plastic snow scenes we used to get in our Christmas stockings every year," he murmured. "What are the little pink things?"

"Opals," Karen said, frowning thoughtfully. "They change color. Sometimes they're almost white. The last few days they've been pink. I've been won-

dering if they might change with the weather or something.''

Matt shrugged, his attention drifting away again.
''Probably the storm coming . . .''

''Yeah,'' she murmured. But even then she was
beginning to wonder if the opals could be quite so
easily explained.

After another hour the room was so jammed with
people, the hostess at the door started holding people
back in the lobby. She let someone new in only when
a guest left for the night. At around ten o'clock Karen
excused herself from Matt long enough to run to the
ladies' room. On her way back, she counted thirty-
four people in line. The party was definitely a success.
Knowing Nona would be pleased, she rushed back
into the party room to tell her.

However, to her surprise, she couldn't find her—
or, for that matter, anyone else she knew. Kurt, Brandon, Matt, and even Jerrie seemed to have been swallowed up by the crush of dancing bodies. In fact, the
crowd had become so dense that, with the exception
of Matt, she couldn't recall actually having seen any
of her friends for over thirty minutes.

Karen inched her way to the food table and sampled
a cracker spread with something creamy that undoubtedly had a zillion calories. Licking her fingers, she
glanced up and at last spotted Matt standing by a window, staring intently across the snowy parking lot. He
wore a worried expression and didn't appear aware of
her as she stepped up beside him.

''What's wrong?'' she asked.

''Nothing.'' With obvious effort he turned away
from the window.

Karen peered out into the dark but could see nothing.
''You sure?''

"Sure I'm sure." He slipped his arm around her shoulders and squeezed. "Listen, I gotta leave for a little bit. But I'll speak to the hostess so she'll let me back in. Since I'm on the planning committee she shouldn't give me a hard time."

"I'll go with you."

"No. Find Nona and hang out with her for a while. I promise this won't take long." He kissed her quickly on the lips. Then, releasing her hand, Matt made his way slowly between dancing couples.

Karen stood still for a moment, then she began to follow him across the room. Standing in the foyer doorway behind the hostess, she watched with an inexplicable sense of anxiety as Matt set his beer can in an ashtray beside the coatrack and searched through the snarl of jackets for his own.

After a while, she smiled dimly, thinking she really should go and help him. He was obviously fuzzy from the beer, having a tough time locating the right coat. However, he finally found the tan jacket and put it on. He must have grown since he bought it, for the sleeves appeared too short for his arms. He didn't seem to notice.

And then he ducked through the door and was gone, and Karen felt strangely bereft.

She lingered near the party room, her eyes glued to the rough barn-plank door that had closed behind Matt with a creak. After another minute, she looked back over her shoulder into the crowd, trying to locate Matt's friends, who had also become hers: Nona, Brandon, and Kurt.

Not one of them was anywhere in sight. Perhaps because she suddenly felt so alone, she reached up and touched Grandma Gee's necklace.

Her hand jumped away! The glass sphere was hot

to her touch. Not merely warm, as it sometimes became after resting between her breasts beneath her sweater. *Hot!* Looking down at her chest, she could see that the crystals inside glowed a brilliant fiery-red.

Danger . . . the opals will warn you of danger! Her grandmother had told her that, but Karen certainly hadn't taken her seriously at the time.

So why did she sense that the whole world was pressing down upon her, crushing her with a sadness so oppressive she could barely force her knees to support her?

Slowly, she moved across the foyer.

"Are you leaving for the night?" the hostess asked with a hopeful smile.

"No. I'll be right back," she answered automatically.

Karen searched among the coats for her parka and found it. With shaking hands, she dragged it on, pulling the hood up over her hair.

I must catch up with Matt! she thought irrationally. The fact that he had told her to remain behind at the party didn't matter. She was convinced that he needed her! But something—a strange force that felt as if it originated from the center of her chest—held her back.

Karen took one step toward the door, then a second. Still, the power seemed to restrain her, and only with the greatest effort was she able to break free of the invisible grip holding her back and burst out of the Wobbly Barn into the winter night.

The wind blew swirls of snow against her cheeks, burning them with icy spurs. She squinted into the crystal billows, trying to spot Matt's car among the herd of silent snow-covered beasts. At last, she found it, but it was empty, and he was nowhere in sight. She looked around. A lone figure was plodding through the storm halfway across the Access Road that ran between the nightclub and a modern condo development.

"Matt, wait up!" Karen called out.

He must not have heard her, for he kept on walking unsteadily, his hands thrust into his pockets for warmth, his head pulled down into his coat collar. In that second, it crossed her mind that this might not be Matt at all, so little of him was visible. Then something caused him to turn and gaze with a puzzled expression down the road. Karen could now see his face, distinctly silhouetted in the white glow of approaching headlights.

From that moment, time moved as if she were trapped in one of those slow-motion scenes in a movie or in an instant replay of Monday night football—a nightmarish contortion of reality. Karen watched, sensing before anything actually happened that the car and her boyfriend were destined to clash—and the battle between flesh and metal would prove no contest.

But he has time to get out of the way! she reasoned intuitively. *He has time to make it the rest of the way across the street before the car reaches him.* Seconds ticked away, but, strangely, Matt seemed in no particular hurry. *Why doesn't he run?*

"Look out!" Karen screamed, her voice swallowed up by the white silence of the snow. The car, unbelievably, picked up speed. "Stop! Oh God, stop!"

As if she'd called out the command to him, Matt swung around, halting in the middle of the road, squinting in Karen's direction. She decided that the cold must not have fully revived his beer-drenched senses.

Any minute now, any minute and they'll see him and slam on the brakes! Karen thought frantically, waving an arm above her head to try to attract the driver's attention and warn Matt.

The lights grew brighter, bigger. Karen could imagine their heat searing into Matt—but of course that was ridiculous. It was twenty degrees outside, and headlights didn't throw heat like that. Maybe she was sensing the driver's emotions, hot and demanding violence, as they seethed behind those blinding high beams.

"Matt, run!" she screamed.

Startled out of his daze, he at last obeyed.

Unfortunately, although he worked his feet energetically through the ankle-deep snow, he didn't appear to make much headway.

Still hoping to wave off the car, Karen stepped into the street. She tried to make out the driver's face behind the rapidly approaching black glaze of windshield. Impossible. She wasn't even able to see much of the vehicle in the dark. She sensed only that it was small and dark colored.

Finally Karen couldn't hold herself back any longer. With her heart in her throat, she dashed into the road, her blond hair whipping out behind her, amber eyes bright with terror, waving her arms crazily above her head like a windmill in a hurricane. Her mouth opened and released an anguished scream, although she never heard it because the racing engine and crunching of tires on the snow-packed road drowned her out.

It was only at the last moment that the beer-clouded haze over Matt's vision must have cleared and he realized his peril, for a knowing expression suddenly came over his face. He was alert, hungry for survival.

Legs pumping, arms flailing, Matt fought for an added burst of speed and ran headlong for the icy drift the plows had pushed up on the far side of the road.

However, the relentless headlights swung, following him, and the engine whined at a higher pitch, as if the driver had floored the accelerator.

Matt tripped, falling hard on the road. Clutching his right knee, he looked up and his horrified eyes reflected the swelling high beams, round and awful and hot. In a final desperate attempt to get out of the way, he rolled and wedged his good leg under him then sprang up, hobbling toward the protection of the four-foot drift.

Karen looked to her right as she ran. One headlight, as big and bold as an August sun, filled her vision. Then cold metal glanced painfully against her knee, knocking her backward. She heard a dull thump followed by a nerve-wrenching crack and looked up to see Matt flying over the hood of the car. She caught a glimpse of his horrified face above her as someone opened the door of the Wobbly Barn, letting out a blast of music and bright light. Then the car passed beneath Matt, and his body hit the icy pavement, landing all sprawled and loose as if his bones had turned to sawdust on impact.

Karen crawled across the snow-covered pavement, tears streaking down her cheeks and falling on his battered face. For a moment, he held onto consciousness. Weakly, Matt stretched out a bloody hand toward her.

I should get the license number! Karen thought vaguely, but she couldn't take her eyes off of Matt for even a second.

He grasped her fingertips weakly and parted scraped lips to mumble a few barely audible words.

"It's all right," she sobbed. "Don't move. Don't try to talk."

And he didn't, not ever again.

Chapter 5

The bedroom remained dark all day and all night, because Karen wouldn't allow anyone to open her shades. She slept nearly all of the time, only crawling out from within her cocoon of warm sheets twice each day to use the private bathroom attached to her room.

Romeo stopped singing, because he thought it was always night. Someone—her mother?—whispered worriedly that he wasn't eating right and moved his cage out of the room.

Karen didn't care. Nothing mattered, least of all whether it was day or night.

Somewhere she'd heard, or read, that people who suffer a traumatic ordeal often fight sleep, for fear of reliving the experience through nightmares. But she clung to the dark emptiness of her room, needing the silence, the solitude—because sounds reminded her of life, and a light in her room encouraged people who wanted to talk about *that night*.

Her parents tiptoed into her room several times every day, gently encouraging her to leave her bed and come downstairs for a bite to eat and some company. Officer Mancini came twice. When she lay passively, refusing to open her eyes or speak to him, he went away again, dissolving back into the gray mists of her semi-consciousness. And there was someone else—someone whose voice seemed less familiar and visited her only once—with questions. Strange questions, much different from those the police asked. They jabbed at her brain like sharp pins, tormenting her, and Karen covered her head with her pillow, forcing herself to sink deeper into her shell of numbing darkness.

"Hi, ya!"

Karen's mouth tasted like wool felt. Her eyelashes were pasted shut. Her legs and arms felt as stiff and brittle as dead tree branches. A hand seized her shoulder and shook her roughly.

"Stop," she grunted.

The hand shook harder.

"Knock it off, ple-e-e-e-ase."

"No way. You are getting up—right this very minute, Karen Henderson." No one could be as pushy as Rosie.

"Get lost, you moron," Karen groaned.

Her blankets were thrown back, and a layer of chilly air wrapped around her bare legs. Karen reached down for the covers, searching with her hands, her eyes still tightly shut. But she couldn't locate the blankets. She pried one eye open a crack and spotted them in a fluffy pink heap on the floor. Rosie stood on the other side of the room, reaching for the bottom of the window shade.

"Don't!" Karen warned, sitting up in bed.

With a loud whoosh, the heavy fabric snapped out of Rosie's fingers, flooding the bedroom with bright winter light. Rosie grinned at her and flung the window up, letting in a gust of frosty air.

"What the hell do you think you're doing?" Karen demanded furiously.

"It stinks in here, and so do you," Rosie informed her. She dusted off her palms as if she'd just finished baking a masterpiece of a cake and turned her attention to Karen's bureau drawers through which she began digging. "I think jeans and a good heavy sweater will do," she mumbled. "And boots, of course."

"I don't want to get dressed." Karen let her body fall back against the pillows and rubbed her eyes. The light hurt them.

"You'll be awfully cold tramping through the woods in your nightie and bare feet," Rosie commented, somehow managing to sound sensible.

"I'm not going for a walk."

"Oh yes you are."

"Mom!" Karen wailed. "Get this maniac out of here!"

"Your mother agreed it would be a wonderful idea to get you out of bed. She's left for the store to pick up some groceries for your newly restored appetite."

"I'm not hungry."

"You will be."

"Oh, good grief!"

Rosie grabbed her by the wrist and yanked her forcibly out of bed. For her size, she was remarkably strong. She shoved underwear, jeans, and a sweater into Karen's arms.

"I am *not* getting dressed," Karen said firmly.

"Right. Not until after you take a shower. Wow, the stench is almost overwhelming! Now—" Rosie crossed her arms over her chest as if she meant business "—into the shower under your own power . . . or *I scrub you!*"

"Oh, for crying out loud . . ."

Reluctantly, Karen tottered into the bathroom. The tile floor felt like a sheet of ice beneath her naked feet. The air smelled faintly of honey and almonds—her favorite shampoo, she remembered. Her balance was off. She bumped into the door as it swung closed behind her.

"Ouch!" She dropped her clothes in a heap and sat down on the toilet seat, holding her head in her hands.

"I don't hear any water running!" Rosie sang through the door.

Karen reached over and turned on both knobs all the way.

After sitting for a couple of minutes in the steam-filled room, she peeked out the door. Rosie was browsing through a stack of magazines, stretched out on her bed, which by now had been stripped of its sheets. With a groan of resignation, Karen pulled off her sticky nightdress and stepped under the hot spray.

The instant the water hit, her skin came alive, and along with it her brain. An image of Matt flashed across her mind like a jagged streak of lightning against the sky on a hot, black summer night. Tears welled up in her eyes, mixing with shower water. But they were tears of anger—no longer those of mourning—tears of fury and disgust and outrage that anyone could do what the driver of that car had done to such a sweet boy.

At least by now, she thought with bitter satisfaction as she turned her face up into the hot spray, *the police must have caught the bastard!*

Karen vowed she wouldn't cry anymore. She soaped up quickly, rinsed, washed her hair twice, then climbed out of the tub. She dressed quickly before opening the bathroom door.

"Want to check behind my ears?" she asked sweetly as she stepped into the bedroom.

Rosie looked up from a *Cosmo* magazine. "I trust you."

Karen noticed that Romeo's cage had been returned to the room. "Mind if I close the window now?" she asked. "Parakeets are very sensitive to drafts."

Rosie nodded. "Want me to blow-dry your hair for you?"

"I think I remember how." Karen sensed that her voice might be a little too harsh. After all, Rosie was just trying to help, and she had to admit that—aside from the painful memory of Matt's loss, which continued to jab at her poor heart—it felt good to be clean and moving around again. "Um . . . you're not serious about that hike, are you?"

Rosie laid the magazine aside. "I am. Dry your hair. We'll have something to eat then get out of here."

Karen took a deep breath. "Rosie," she said softly, "I appreciate what you're trying to do, but I really don't think I can keep anything down just yet. I'll go for a walk with you, but no food."

"Fine by me."

They hiked down the path behind the big house and into the woods. About a half mile along, Rosie chose a shortcut down a hill and through a thick stand of pine and chalky-barked birch trees. Karen followed and was surprised when they came out at a little convenience store on Route Four. Rosie purchased Twinkies, devil's food cupcakes, and a quart of milk, all of which looked gross to Karen.

"You don't have to eat anything," Rosie reassured her when they were outside again, "but I'm starving."

Karen had no intention of eating. However, she couldn't help watching Rosie devour one pack of the sponge cake treats and move on to the cupcakes with enthusiasm. The two girls were halfway back to the house when an undeniable urge for one nibble of chocolate cake hit Karen.

"Are you planning on eating the second cupcake?" Karen asked meekly.

Rosie shrugged. "Unless someone else does, I will." She smiled. "Go ahead. Take it."

The moist, rich texture filled her mouth. Karen finished off the cake in two more bites.

"This isn't the first time you came to see me, is it?" she asked, licking frosting from her fingers.

"No. It's the third."

"I don't remember."

"I know."

Karen frowned. What else had she missed? "Who came besides you?"

Rosie thought for a minute as they climbed the hill. "Nobody while I was around. Your mom mentioned that the doctor stopped in a couple times."

Had it been his voice asking questions that made her want to sink deeper into her isolation? Somehow Karen doubted it.

They stepped out of the woods and circled back to the house. To her surprise, Kurt was sitting on the front steps, waiting for them.

Seeing him brought a lump to Karen's throat, and she stopped short. His pale eyes fixed on her for a second, then dropped away as if the contact was as painful for him as it was for her. What was it like to lose your best friend? Until that moment she thought she understood—but then she'd known Matt only for a month. Kurt and Matt had been close for years.

"Hi, Kurt!" Rosie called out, forever cheerful.

"Hi." He gave her a brief nod, then turned to Karen

as she climbed the steps, gripping the cast-iron railing to steady herself. Her knees still felt spongy from days of disuse. "I want to talk to you," he said.

"Okay."

"In private."

"I was just leaving," Rosie announced. "My mom expects me home to help with dinner."

"If you'd rather I not stay—" Kurt began as Rosie walked down the driveway.

"No," Karen said quickly. "Come on in."

He followed her into the living room. It was a sunny room with freshly hung Laura Ashley rose-patterned wallpaper, soft green brocade drapes, and an Oriental carpet her mother had bought at an auction while they still lived in New York. Karen sat on one end of the pretty Victorian love seat, Kurt on the other. Aside from her bedroom, this was her favorite spot in the house. One thing you could say for her mother, she knew how to decorate a room.

"I won't stay long," Kurt murmured. "I just thought you'd want to know—before you read about it in the paper."

"Know what?"

"The police have dropped the investigation into Matt's death."

Karen's mouth fell open, and for a second she couldn't find her voice. "No!" she croaked at last. "That's impossible." Ever since arising from her deep blue funk, she'd assumed that the police had nailed the driver. Hadn't Mancini promised her that he would as her father bundled her off in his cushy sedan?

"I'm afraid so," said Kurt. "Today's newspaper has a short story about the accident. The police believe Matt was a hit-and-run victim, and the driver was probably someone from out of town who'd had too much to drink. Whoever it was must have taken off as soon as they realized what they'd done."

A thick red smog descended over her eyes. Karen couldn't remember ever being angrier. "I don't believe it! They aren't even going to try to find his murderer?"

Kurt looked down at his hands. "Murder? Why do you call it that?"

"Because whoever was behind that wheel is a cold-blooded killer."

Kurt's cool blue eyes met hers questioningly. "Maybe the driver never saw Matt . . . if he was drunk enough and all. . . ."

Karen opened her lips, then closed them again, staring at him.

"What were you going to say just now?" he asked, his voice a hoarse whisper.

"Just that . . . that's impossible."

"Why?"

Karen considered for a moment. "Because the car swerved more than once. It looked as if it were chasing him down."

"Maybe the driver was trying to avoid him and just guessed the wrong direction."

Karen shook her head firmly. Although she'd never forget the agony of those few minutes just before that speeding car hit Matt, there admittedly were details about the night that she'd been unable to recall for Mancini, and others she simply hadn't been in a good position to observe. Gradually a few of those she had seen were becoming clearer.

"No," she said. "The driver of that car was *trying* to hit Matt. Matt didn't have a chance. Oh, God!" She lost her fragile grip on her emotions and burst into tears. "You didn't see. You weren't there, Kurt. . . . Matt tried to get away! I watched him run. . . . He fell. . . . He got up and ran again, but . . . but—''

Kurt slid across the cushions and pulled her into his arms to stroke her back comfortingly, over and over. ''I'm sorry, Karen. I guess you really loved him.''

She nodded silently, unsure if love was really the right word for what she'd felt toward Matt, and sobbed softly into Kurt's sweater.

''Could you see the driver?'' he asked after a few minutes. ''Anything of a face at all?''

''No . . . nothing. I would have told the police.''

''What about the car? The make? Color?''

Karen choked back the hot, salty mucous clogging her throat. Her head was pounding. ''It was so dark that night, the snow coming down really heavy. Mostly, I just saw headlights.'' She hesitated, thinking. ''But I had a feeling that it was a small car, and dark colored.''

''You didn't by any chance get a license plate number, did you?''

''If I had, don't you think the police would have found the driver by now?'' she snapped.

''I guess so,'' he muttered disconsolately.

''I'm sorry, I don't mean to be bitchy. I just feel so useless.''

He looked at her for a moment longer as if wanting to ask her something else. . . . Then he must have reconsidered.

Karen pulled back slightly and gazed up at his strong Nordic features: rigid jaw, high cheekbones, washed blue eyes. She wiped beneath her own eyes with the back of one hand. ''Were you here before?''

''Before?''

''Did you come up to my room to see me after . . . after that night?''

''No,'' he said quickly, but there was a slight catch

in his voice that made her not trust his answer. "I called twice," he added quickly. "Your mother said you weren't able to talk."

Karen peered at him speculatively through tear-dampened lashes. "Someone came into my room and asked me questions. I don't remember answering them. . . . But I might have."

"Probably the police," he suggested. "They must have been trying to track down the hit-and-run car. You were the only witness."

"I guess I wasn't much help," she admitted bitterly.

Kurt shrugged as if to say he understood, but his tight expression and downcast eyes made her doubt that he did. Suddenly, she felt overwhelmed with guilt and knew she had to do something.

Karen leaped up from the love seat and ran out of the living room then upstairs. She quickly checked the phone book in her bedroom for an address and snatched up her purse from the bureau where it had lain since the night of the accident.

"Where are you going?" Kurt asked, looking up at her from the hallway as she tore back down the stairs.

"To see Officer Mancini at the state police barracks in Rutland. I have to convince him that he should reopen Matt's case."

Kurt reached out and stopped her as she started to brush past him. His eyes had turned hard.

"What?" she asked.

"Do you really want to do this, Karen?"

"I don't understand," she murmured, disturbed by his attitude. "Don't you want the police to get the person who did this?"

Kurt looked flustered for a second, and when he at last spoke his accent had thickened, his Rs rolling in his throat. "Right. Sure, I do."

"Then let go of me."

He moved aside, releasing her arm.

A moment later, Karen backed her car out of the old-fashioned wooden garage for the first time in over a week. She watched Kurt through her rearview mirror as he climbed into his own car and drove off. Then she turned the convertible around in the wide driveway and headed for Rutland and the state police barracks.

Lieutenant Mancini was much the same as she remembered him—tall, wide through the chest and shoulders. Unlike TV police detectives who often carried around a beer gut, he had a flat, hard-looking stomach that appeared as if he did a couple hundred sit-ups each day to maintain it. He could have posed for an ad for the U.S. Marines. He had that tough, don't-give-me-any-crap look about him.

"Technically, we haven't closed the case," he told her.

"Then you think there's still a possibility," Karen said carefully, "that you'll find the driver of the car that struck Matt?"

Mancini gave her a long look. "It's possible."

"But not likely?"

He sat on the edge of his desk and gestured at a visitor's chair. Karen sat down, eye level with the large steel gray desk and Mancini's formidable knee.

"To be frank," he said slowly, "whether or not we find the driver depends at least somewhat upon you, Karen. Do you have anything new to tell me? Something you've remembered that might have slipped your mind on the night of the accident?"

Karen shut her eyes for a moment. Oh, how she wished there was something. A license plate number.

A description of the car. A glimpse of the driver. Anything!

But all she saw on the black screen of her closed lids was blood on the snow and the ravaged body of her boyfriend.

"No," she whispered hoarsely, at last opening her eyes. "There's nothing more."

"Too bad." He held his hands open in a gesture of helplessness.

"What about the car?" she persisted. "There must have been some damage done to it. It had to have been going fifty or sixty when it hit Matt." She shuddered, hearing in her mind the sound of his bones crunching against the bumper.

Mancini nodded. "My men erected blockades on every road leading out of town. They stopped and checked each car that came through directly after the accident. None of the vehicles showed any signs of having been involved in a hit-and-run. And it's been ten days since the accident, but no garages in central Vermont have accepted any body repair jobs matching the sort of damage we'd expect from striking a person at that speed. Somehow, the one we're after must have slipped out of town."

Karen hesitated before asking cautiously, "Is there anything that indicates this might *not* have been an accident?"

"You mean someone intentionally killed Matthew Welch?"

Karen nodded, feeling a dull tug of disgust in her stomach. Anyone capable of such a thing was an animal—worse.

"Nothing I've seen indicates premeditated murder." Mancini studied her expression, leaning forward with his wide hands planted on his knees. "Why would you even think it's a possibility?"

"A feeling. Something happened . . . I don't know . . . the way the driver steered toward Matt even when he tried to get out of the way. It was as if the car had become a living thing . . . stalking its prey."

Mancini shook his head. "A drunk behind the wheel can't drive in a straight line any better than he can walk one. There were a lot of parties going on all up and down the Access Road on race night." He leveled a solemn gaze at her. "I understand that somebody smuggled booze into your party at the Wobbly Barn. The autopsy showed your boyfriend had been drinking."

"I don't see what that has to do with it," she said impatiently. "Whether Matt was drunk or sober makes no difference. And besides, the car didn't come from the Wobbly Barn parking lot."

He observed her solemnly. "Are you certain, Karen? You were in shock that night. You admitted that you were confused, only recalling a few details because of how suddenly it happened."

"I know," she murmured, gazing down at her purse in her lap. "So, you don't think that anyone was trying to kill Matt?"

"No." Mancini gave her a practiced smile, the kind meant to encourage small children or ill people. She'd seen her father use it enough times to recognize it.

"All right," she said, standing up to leave. "I guess I must be imagining things."

But she didn't believe a word of it.

Nona opened her front door and stared blankly at Karen for a full ten seconds as if she didn't recognize her. Then she threw her arms around her, and the two girls hugged until they were both breathless.

"Oh, God, Karen. I heard you'd had a nervous breakdown and weren't able to see anyone! You all right?"

"Yes," she said, but there was a quiver in her voice. Karen gently pushed Nona back and gave her what was intended to be a reassuring smile but probably looked as strained as it was. "Got a minute?"

"Sure. Come in." Nona led her into the living room, which was a cozy, country style parlor with hand-embroidered cushions and calico upholstery. Nona's schoolbooks were spread out on the braided rug. Karen preferred to do her work on the floor, too. Nona waved at a big armchair and curled up on the sofa herself.

"Is Brandon here?" Karen asked.

"No. He just left for work."

She had wanted to talk to both of them at the same time, but this would have to do for now. Drawing a deep breath, she dove in. "Where were you when Matt was killed?"

Nona blinked as if startled. "You know where I was."

"It's important, Nona. Please. *Exactly* where were you? In the party room? In the lobby? Outside in the parking lot?"

Nona huffed. "You sound like the police, I swear. Okay, I was inside the Wobbly Barn, and best I can figure I was in the ladies' room, trying to avoid Frank Roselli."

"Avoid him?"

"He'd been following me all over the place. He was being a pest."

"I thought you liked him."

"I do. But he was coming on awful strong. It just made me feel creepy."

Karen had a strange thought. "Have you ever had a boyfriend?"

"Sure, lots of them. Boys naturally feel comfortable around me. Maybe that's because of Brandon, because we're so close."

"But being a pal with a boy is different from being his girlfriend," Karen pointed out.

"You mean sex? I've never been interested in *that* sort of relationship. I suppose I will be, someday . . . when the right boy comes along. I just think that Frank isn't the one."

Karen thought she sounded very reasonable. After all, being a virgin wasn't a crime, and, more importantly, Nona's love life wasn't uppermost in Karen's mind.

"I just came from talking to the police," she said.

"The police? Why?"

"About Matt, of course."

Nona gave her a searching look. "Do you think that's a good idea—to keep dwelling on that night?"

"I tried to blank it out, but that didn't work," Karen admitted. She took another deep breath. "Nona, are you sure you didn't see anything that night?"

"How could I have from inside the toilet?"

"What about Brandon? Where was he?"

"I don't know. You'll have to ask him."

But you do know. You know everything your brother does! The thought slipped through her mind.

Nona continued. "You worry me, Karen. You're becoming obsessed with this accident. Sure it was tragic. But Matt was Brandon's best friend. How do you think my brother will feel if you pester him with questions about that night? You should have seen him skiing the Challenge the next day. His time was absolutely terrible. I don't think he even placed in the top twenty!''

Karen stared at Nona in disbelief. "Brandon raced on the Sunday after Matt died?''

"Well, it's not like there was anything he could *do* about it!'' Nona snapped in her brother's defense. "Besides, Kurt skied, too—only he won.''

Karen frowned. Kurt hadn't mentioned the race or his victory when he'd come to her house earlier in the day. She'd assumed that the second day of the Challenge had been cancelled. Even if it hadn't been, going ahead with the race seemed a cold-hearted thing to do while their friend lay in a morgue!

"Karen,'' Nona whispered, pulling her out of her dark thoughts, "there's nothing any of us can do.'' Tears trembled in the corners of her sad eyes. "We all loved him, but we have to let him go.''

But did we all *love him?* Karen wondered. *Or, was there one exception—someone who wanted Matt Welch dead?*

Karen had to think, and she'd never been able to concentrate on an empty stomach. After leaving Nona's house, she pulled over at the Pizza Attack and walked inside. The restaurant smelled of warm yeast, beer, garlic, and tomatoes. Her mouth instantly responded by watering.

A familiar stocky young man with dark hair and a Mediterranean complexion worked behind the counter. "Can I help y— Oh, hi, Karen.''

"Hello, Frank.'' She looked up at the lighted menu hanging over his head. "Give me a slice of pepperoni pizza . . . no, two slices, and a diet cola, to eat here.''

"Thin or thick crust?''

"Thick."

Frank placed two triangles of dough mounded with cheese and circles of pepperoni on a paper plate. He slid it into the warmer, then turned away to fill a cup with ice and soda. "I haven't seen you in school lately," he commented in a quiet voice.

"No, I haven't been there."

"Are you coming back?" She couldn't see his expression, but his voice sounded taut.

"Sure. I just wasn't feeling too great."

"That's understandable." He swung around and set the soda in front of her with a smile that didn't seem to match his solemn voice. "Good to see you again."

Something suddenly occurred to Karen. "The night of the accident—you were working here, weren't you?"

"Here and making deliveries. Race nights we're always swamped."

"Was your car running?"

Frank hesitated, giving her a sideways look. "As a matter of fact it wouldn't start. I had to borrow one."

"Oh." A heavy feeling settled in her stomach. "Your dad's?"

"A friend's. My father was driving his own. One delivery man couldn't handle all the orders on his own that night."

"Whose car did you borrow?" she asked, holding her breath.

The muscles in his forearms stiffened, although his expression remained neutral. "Just a friend's. I didn't exactly get permission, and he might get ticked off if he found out."

"No problem." She forced a smile. "Listen, I changed my mind. Could you put my slices in a box? I think I'll eat at home."

A minute later, Karen crossed the gravel parking area toward her car with a lot on her mind. She couldn't stop thinking about the insane way Frank drove or wondering whose car he had borrowed on the night of the party . . . or what condition it was in now.

That night Karen propped herself up on her bed with four pillows. Romeo perched one-footed on her shoulder, twittering his soothing sleepy-time song in her ear. She stroked his silky wings and whistled at him.

Karen had intended to read herself to sleep. She'd slept so much in the past days she wasn't sure she could drift off naturally, and the book—a translation of a Greek tragedy for her English class—was chosen specifically to make her drowsy.

She put Romeo back in his cage and had actually started to doze off when she heard an odd scraping sound. It seemed to be coming from her father's office in the basement. Suddenly alert, she made her way to the top of the stairs and listened. When she'd been a little girl, her father had instructed her how to call the police should someone break into their house. Doctors' homes were often the targets of addicts searching for drugs.

Karen listened a little longer, and only then did she realize the sounds weren't coming from the basement at all. They were somewhere outside of the house— but close, very close.

Possibly a wild animal had ventured out of the woods looking for food. On several occasions she'd seen raccoon prints around the garbage cans beside the garage. If she woke up her parents or called the police and it was only a raccoon, she'd feel like an idiot.

Karen tiptoed downstairs, took a coat from the hall

closet, and, still pulling it over her nightdress, rummaged through a kitchen drawer for a flashlight. At the back door, she stepped into boots and then out into the night.

Pointing the yellow beam over crisp white snow, she spotted the old raccoon tracks, worn shallow by the wind, barely visible. She froze in her tracks as the scraping sound came to her from inside the garage.

Holding her breath, Karen moved closer. Through the frosty window in the side wall of the garage, she could see a dim light. She inched closer, her heart in her throat, and peered cautiously through the glass. The old wooden garage doors had already been pushed wide open, and an unidentifiable figure, bundled in heavy winter clothes, was climbing into her car.

Without considering the wisdom of what she was about to do, Karen ran around the corner and into the garage. "Hey, that's my car!" she screeched.

The intruder either didn't hear or simply ignored her, for the engine started up with a roar and then raced loudly.

What kind of a dumb car thief is this? she wondered. *The whole town will hear the getaway!*

Karen bolted for the driver's side and wrenched open the door. Rosie looked up at her with huge, shocked eyes.

"What do you think you're doing?" Karen screamed indignantly. "Get your ass out of my car!"

Rosie's eyes filled with tears. "Oh, I'm so sorry. I thought I'd just borrow it for a couple hours, then have it back before morning. . . . Before anyone knew."

"I don't recall your asking," Karen said coldly. She reached across Rosie, flicked off the ignition, and pulled out the key. "Where did you get this?"

"I had a copy made."

"How?" Karen demanded.

"When I came to visit you one time, I took your key from your purse, meaning to use it to drive to visit Chuck. But I couldn't make myself do it, you were so sick and . . ." She gulped back her tears, gazing up at Karen pleadingly as she stepped out of the car. "But then I thought I'd just get a copy made, for an emergency. So I did. I put the original key back in your purse today."

"Where were you going?"

"To visit Chuck, of course. Oh, geez, you can't believe how much I miss him."

Karen swallowed over the lump in her throat. "I know how it feels to miss someone," she whispered tightly.

Rosie looked horrified. "Oh, I'm so sorry. Matt. Of course, you must miss him." She grabbed Karen around the shoulders and hugged her hard. "I'm such a jerk. Poor Matt. Poor, poor Matt."

Karen shoved her back to arm's length. "Where were you the night of the accident?"

"With Chuck, at his dorm." Despite her attempt to look contrite, Rosie's eyes sparkled mischievously.

"You weren't at the Wobbly Barn party?"

"I got tired of hanging around in line, so at about nine-thirty I left."

"How did you get there?" Karen demanded, unconvinced.

"I thumbed."

"You didn't borrow my car that night, did you?"

"No, I told you I hadn't done it before." Rosie looked at her. "You believe me, don't you?"

Karen's head felt fuzzy; her nerves buzzed as if sounding an alarm. She'd never actually seen Rosie at the Wobbly Barn that night, and she had only Rosie's word that she was already at Green Mountain College at the time of the accident. Nevertheless, she forced a small smile. "Of course I believe you." Karen dropped her key into the pocket of her robe. "Look, it's late, you shouldn't be driving to the college now. Tomorrow I'll take you."

Rosie blinked, mopping at her tears with her knuckles. "You will?"

"Sure. Now go home and get some sleep."

Rosie nodded and obediently walked out of the garage and down the driveway toward the street.

Watching her go, Karen stood in the open doorway. When Rosie was out of sight, she reached over for the light switch. But something made her hesitate before turning off the bare overhead bulb. Slowly she swiveled around and, with an itchy feeling in the pit of her stomach, walked to the front of her car—praying she wouldn't find what she envisioned.

The metal grillwork and bumper were shiny and clean of all but a thin spray of salt from driving around during the day. And, for a moment, Karen felt relief seeping into her veins. But something made her stoop down and run her fingers along the metal. Two marked depressions marred the smooth surface beneath the fine coating of grit. And just above them on the front of the hood, before it curved and flattened out on top, was a third and deeper indentation.

That's where Matt's head hit! she thought, feeling sick to her stomach.

Chapter 6

Karen sank back onto her heels, her stomach heaving, her head spinning.

No! This isn't happening! she thought wildly. It just wasn't possible that *her* car had been the one that had killed Matt. And yet—

Yet, now that the suspicion had entered her mind, she had trouble dismissing it. The damage to the front end of the convertible was recent, she had no memory of it happening, and the position of those dents seemed too perfect to be coincidental.

Was it possible?

Headlights disembodied in the dark night. During those terrifying few minutes that had seemed an eternity, she'd never actually *seen* the car. It had appeared out of the blizzard as a speeding, demonic shadow, tracking Matt down as unfailingly as if it had been a heat-sensitive missile. It really could have been hers!

However, the convertible had been shut up in the garage when Nona picked her up. She was sure of that; she'd run out to get her gloves from the front seat just before Nona arrived.

"Oh, God!" Karen moaned, her legs collapsing

beneath her. She sat abruptly on the cold, oil-stained cement. "*My* car! Matt!" She covered her eyes with her hands. Her whole body shook.

For what seemed like forever, Karen felt unable to move. Gradually the cold seeped into her bones through the cement. She grew conscious of the hard floor biting into her ankles and knees, and somehow she struggled to her feet and staggered toward the house.

In the darkness of her bedroom she lay on her bed, telling herself that anyone could have gotten into the unlocked garage, used her car, then replaced it. Any stranger who happened by. Which was true. However, no vagrant or tourist could possibly have chanced on *her* particular house, *her* very own car, and run over *her* boyfriend, then carefully cleaned off the bloody bumper and returned the vehicle to her home.

Too many coincidences. She didn't believe in coincidence. Things usually happened for a reason.

The only solution she could accept—no matter what the police thought or how incredible it might sound— was that Matt's killer had planned his death. He, or she, was someone Karen knew and who knew her and Matt very well—well enough to use her to murder him.

A suspicious voice nudged her subconscious. Sometime before Matt was run down, Karen had lost track of their friends at the party. Kurt. Brandon and Nona. Jerrie had been a standout on the dance floor early in the evening, evaporating into the crowd as the night wore on. She might have been missing for as much as an hour, now that Karen really stopped to think about it.

And what about Frank Roselli? He hadn't been at the party at all; he even admitted to borrowing a car that night to make his deliveries. And he'd seemed very uneasy about telling her whose it had been. Was his only reason for keeping that information to himself fear of angering a friend?

And last of all, there was Rosie Geer, desperate to visit her college boyfriend. Desperate enough tonight to try to steal Karen's car and drive it without a license. Perhaps, Karen thought grimly, this wasn't the first time.

Kurt pulled on clean underwear and tossed his dirty clothes into the gym bag on the floor.

"Sure you haven't forgotten anything?" Brandon asked, glancing around his living room as Kurt tugged on his jeans.

"I don't think so. I didn't bring much."

Last night, like so many others before, Kurt had crashed on the couch. Since Brandon had his own apartment over the garage, no one objected. Good thing, too. Some nights the tension between Kurt and his father in their Winter Crest condo across the street from the Wobbly Barn was so thick, Kurt couldn't stand being in the same house with him.

"Thanks again for the bed," he murmured.

Brandon lit up a cigarette and crossed his heels on the coffee table. "No problem. Anytime." He squinted up at Kurt. "You really hate your old man, don't you?"

"Hate him?" Kurt laughed tightly. "Maybe that's not quite the right word. I just sort of wish he didn't exist." He hesitated, unsure whether he should confide any further in Brandon. But since Matt was gone, there just wasn't anyone else he was close enough to. "In a way . . ." he continued slowly, his throat tightening with regret, ". . . I'm sorry our relationship is so strained. It's not as if he drinks or beats me or anything. In fact, Heinz always tries to give me everything I need, everything I even remotely want. Maybe it's because he tries so hard, too hard. . . ." Kurt shrugged, confused. "I don't know. . . ."

"Weird," mumbled Brandon.

Kurt walked over to the window and looked out over the drifts of white snow. A chill ran up his spine as he envisioned another drift, another time very long ago. He'd seen a photograph. . . . Or maybe the drift was in some place he'd really been. He couldn't be sure. The image seemed as if it were something out of another lifetime.

"I think it's more than that," Kurt muttered darkly.

"Like what?"

"I'm not sure. Something that was a secret between my parents."

"You never talk about your mother," Brandon pointed out.

"I know. I think about her a lot, though," Kurt whispered, his heart suddenly feeling heavy in his chest. "I think it must have been something Heinz did that made my mother take me away. I was only about two years old then."

"That's rough, but at least you had one parent left," Brandon said sympathetically.

"Yeah, but until my mother died years later, I thought my father was dead. That was what she'd told me—that he'd been killed in an accident. Anyway, somehow Heinz heard about her death and sent for me. He was, in fact, very much alive and owned a small construction firm in the United States."

"Lucky you. Instant rich boy." Brandon chuckled dryly.

Kurt shrugged. "The money didn't make any difference. In fact, I hated Heinz for being well-off. Somehow, it didn't seem right. . . . He was rich, and my mother . . .''

Brandon blew out a long puff of cigarette smoke and squinted through the dirty haze, looking puzzled. It occurred to Kurt that Brandon might not be able to understand how he felt about his mother. Brandon and Nona had been raised by an aunt and had hardly known their own parents.

''What the hell is that supposed to mean?'' Brandon finally asked. ''Like, *he* was alive, your mom was dead, and it should have been the other way around?''

Kurt swallowed hard and nodded. ''I know that sounds brutal. But sometimes that one idea burns into my brain like a hot coal . . . until I think I might go crazy from wanting to rewrite history.''

Even now his heart remained hardened against his father. Why that was Kurt couldn't quite put his finger on. So today, like most days, he would go home only when he was sure Heinz was busy at the building site. Or he'd wait until his father was asleep for the night. Actually, Brandon had come painfully close to the truth. Kurt was terrified of what he might do if left alone with the old man.

Clutching an enormous wooden hall pass in one hand, Nona strode down the west corridor of Killington High during third period. She was in front of a sociology classroom when Kurt rushed out of the door, almost knocking her over. He grabbed her arm with his free hand, just managing to keep her from crashing into the lockers.

''Hey, Kurt!'' She laughed.

''Sorry,'' he mumbled, looking distracted. ''I wasn't thinking about where I was going.''

"It's all right."

"Where are you headed?" he asked.

"The newspaper office," she said with a sigh. "Mr. Everett is trying to put together a special issue in honor of Matt."

Kurt's eyes brightened. "Really? I have some good photos of him at last year's track meet with Rutland. Think he'd want to use them?"

"I don't know," Nona said, frowning.

"What's wrong?"

She shrugged and resumed walking. Kurt fell into step beside her. "I'm not sure this special issue is a good idea, that's all," she said finally.

"I don't see why not," Kurt objected. "It's the least the school can do for Matt after all the recognition he brought to Killington."

Matt had been the A-Division state cross-country champ for the past two years. *But he wasn't able to outrun a damn car!* Nona thought morbidly.

"His death has been hard enough on his friends," Nona said in a hushed voice, dropping her glance as her eyes threatened to fill with tears. She stopped abruptly in the middle of the crowded hall and looked up at him. "I'm not sure all of us can take being reminded of that night."

"But we can't just do nothing."

"Think about poor Karen," Nona suggested. "How will she feel seeing Matt's picture plastered all over a special edition? Matt hitting the ribbon at the state meet. Matt dancing with me at last year's prom—"

"That's right, I forgot you two went to the prom together." For some reason that seemed to surprise Kurt.

"As friends," Nona reminded him, "because neither of us wanted to go stag."

Kurt smiled dimly. "I seem to remember that Matt was pretty excited about being your date. I always wondered if he had a crush on you."

Nona considered this for a minute. "I doubt it. Anyway," she continued briskly, "I'm worried about Karen. She wants to prolong the investigation for some reason, and I just don't think it's healthy. She'll hurt herself in the end."

Kurt looked thoughtful. "It's possible, I guess, for her to become obsessed with Matt's death." The bell rang, and he hesitated before mumbling something more.

"What?" Nona demanded, unable to hear him over the sudden swell of voices and slamming of locker doors.

"I said, sometimes I wonder why . . . you know . . . why Karen chose Matt instead of me." He shuffled his feet, looking embarrassed that he'd brought it up.

Nona moved closer and looked compassionately up into his eyes. "You really do like her, don't you?"

Kurt took a deep breath, then nodded. "I guess I've been crazy about her since the first day I saw her. I just didn't realize it until Matt and Karen had become an item."

"Well, if you like her that much, do her a favor," Nona advised. "Talk to her. Try to calm her down a little. Encourage her to let go of the dead. It's for the best," Nona finished sensibly, "for both of you."

"I suppose you're right," Kurt mumbled, staring at the floor. "It's very good advice in fact. Maybe if I'd taken it years ago, my father and I would have worked things out."

"You see?" Nona said with a grin.

"I have a free period this afternoon," Kurt thought out loud. "I might be able to convince Karen to go skiing with me after school. We could talk then.''

"You're a sweetheart, Kurt," Nona cooed. She lightly touched his cheek with her fingertips. "Thanks a bunch."

Karen smiled wanly at Kurt and propped the ends of her skis in the snow. "I don't know why I let you talk me into this," she said. "I have so much schoolwork to make up."

"You need a break," he assured her. "An hour's worth of physical exertion will help you concentrate better."

"I suppose."

"Besides, how can you pass up a free private lesson with the best instructor at Killington?" Kurt teased.

That got a grin out of her. "Guess I can't." She turned to look at the trail map posted beside them. "So, where do we start? This looks like an interesting trail."

He followed her finger as it traced a thin black line on the map's surface. "You might be ready for the Devil's Fiddle by the end of next year, if you ski every day. For now we'll pick something a little less challenging than a black diamond trail."

"Did Matt ski the Devil's Fiddle?" she asked.

"Sure. He, Brandon, and I used to take a run on it now and then on a dare. But I wouldn't allow even my advanced students on the Devil's Fiddle. It's incredibly steep with dangerous terrain."

"Like rocks, and trees, and cliffs?"

"Exactly. If you fall on the Fiddle, the ski patrol just picks up the pieces at the bottom. It's almost impossible to stop once you lose control on a mountain that steep."

Karen wrinkled her nose in distaste. That didn't

sound like much fun at all. "Let's try another slope," she said.

Kurt laughed. "Good idea. Put on your skis. We'll move over to the Needle's Eye. There will be fewer people there than here on Snowshed where you were skiing before."

In fact, from the map it looked as if they would never run out of trails. Killington was actually a resort composed of six mountains, connected by a maze of trails. Winding up and down and around these peaks were over a hundred beautiful ski trails of varying difficulty.

Karen and Kurt took the double chair lift to the top of the Needle's Eye. When the chairs started to revolve around the huge metal cog to begin their trip back down, Kurt pushed himself up from the seat and slid on his skis down a gentle slope. A little shakily at first, Karen followed him, her skis scraping softly over the snow as she shaped them into a wedge.

Kurt glanced over his shoulder. "You're doing great. You had a good teacher."

She smiled weakly. "Matt was very patient. I'm fine as long as the hill doesn't get much steeper than this."

Kurt slowed down and waited for her to catch up, then gave her a few pointers. "Put a little more bend in your knees and keep your weight centered."

He pushed off with his poles as she snowplowed down the gradual slope, the tips of her skis angled toward each other to control the speed of her descent.

"Want to go a little faster?" he asked. "It's more fun."

"What if I can't stop?" Up ahead the trail appeared to take a rather dizzying drop.

"If you're worried about getting up too much speed,

hold onto my waist. We'll go down together."

Kurt maneuvered in front of her, angling his skis into the V she'd made with hers.

Karen laughed nervously. "Are you sure this will work?"

"I do it all the time with my students. Trust me."

Trust me. Why did those words sound so familiar? It was almost as if Kurt had asked her that before, though she couldn't recall when. Or as if they'd come out of a dream. She glanced down at her necklace. This was the first time she'd worn it since the accident. Her mother, undressing her at home that night, must have removed it and placed it in Karen's jewelry box where she'd found it only this morning. The opals were a pale, shimmery blue-green, as though they were telling her that she'd be safe with Kurt.

Smiling, Karen clasped her arms around his waist, and they glided off at a nice crisp pace down the mountainside. She squealed as the sharp winter wind nibbled at her face, and she buried her cheek against the shoulder of Kurt's ski suit. Through the fabric she could feel the length of his body tighten against her chest, his warmth seep through their thick outer clothes.

An image flashed through her mind—Kurt holding her, caressing her, kissing her tenderly. Almost in the same second she saw Matt's face and felt dreadful for enjoying her daydream.

Unaware of her torn emotions, Kurt turned around and grinned at Karen as they slid to a stop near the base lodge.

"You liked that," he observed, pulling his goggles from over his eyes and onto his forehead.

"I *loved* it!" She laughed out loud, her cheeks tingling pleasantly in the cold air, her vision bright in the sun's glare off the snow. "Can we do it again? A couple more runs and I think I'll be able to try it on my own."

Kurt put an arm around her. "Brave girl. I'm proud of you."

Karen giggled, feeling herself blush. Then she looked up into Kurt's eyes and saw a mirror of her own desire from a moment earlier. His smile dropped away, replaced by an intense expression around his lips. His usually pale blue eyes turned shades darker. And she knew that he was going to kiss her.

Karen forgot about her loyalty to Matt, about the last few terrible weeks, about schoolwork, moving from New York, the mystery of the necklace, and . . . everything. Kurt quickly bent down and touched his lips to hers—holding them there for a long, sweet kiss. As her mouth warmed under his, she felt as if her whole body was melting in his arms.

Karen let out a little whimper and opened her eyes to find Kurt staring at her with a look of surprise.

"I . . . I'm sorry," he mumbled, releasing her and backing away as if she were made of steam and he'd been scalded. "I didn't plan to get you out here alone to come on to you or anything."

"I know," she said softly.

"I really like you, Karen," he mumbled awkwardly.

"It wasn't just a game with you?"

Kurt looked shocked. "A game? You mean, you found out about Nona's challenge? I'd forgotten all about that." He looked apologetic. "Well, it was never a game for me. I thought you were great. But so did Matt, and he wasn't as lucky with girls so I just sort of—"

"Let him have me?" Karen finished. "As if I were a book or a chair or something?"

"No!" he barked out. "It wasn't like that at all."

She narrowed her eyes at him. "Somehow I don't picture you giving up on anything that easily, Kurt. Don't get me wrong, it's not that I think I'm that special or anything. But you and Matt and Brandon always competed over everything, didn't you?"

He looked confused. "Yeah, sure. But it was all in good fun."

"Always?" Karen asked, her curiosity growing. She was no longer thinking about the two boys competing for her. Another sort of competition, a far more dangerous one, was on her mind. "Sometimes, didn't things get out of hand? Like at the mogul trials?"

"We all like winning. We play hard. There's nothing wrong with that," Kurt objected.

"The day after Matt died, both you and Brandon raced." She hesitated, weighing her words. "And *you* won."

"Hey! Hold on there!" Kurt gasped. "You don't think I'd ever hurt one of my friends just to put him out of a race, do you?"

Karen looked at him thoughtfully, then glanced away from his sharp blue eyes. She jammed her pole tips down behind her heels to release the bindings and stepped off of her skis. "No. Of course not."

"Then what do you think?" Kurt demanded.

Karen picked up her skis and started crunching across the snow in her boots toward the parking lot.

Kurt didn't bother removing his own skis but skated across the thin layer of packed snow, sliding in front of her to block her escape. "Karen," he whispered hoarsely. "Say something."

She bit down on her lip, trying to get a grip on her

102

swirling emotions. "I don't know what to think, to be honest," she said quietly. "But I'm sure of one thing—someone intentionally ran Matt down."

"You're just searching for someone to blame."

"No," Karen said firmly. She glanced down at the opals again. They were still shining a gentle blue, almost the color of Kurt's troubled eyes. She looked up at him wondering if she dared trust the stones, or Kurt. "Come with me," she murmured. "I have something to show you."

Chapter 7

They stood side by side in the parking lot below Killington Peak. Karen watched Kurt's face for any sign of reaction as he crouched to study the front bumper of her car. His expression gave away about as much of his thoughts as if he'd been an ice sculpture.

"This could have happened some other time. You just didn't notice it," he suggested, sounding hopeful.

"My car was in perfect condition," Karen insisted. "It didn't have a scratch on it before the night of the party."

"Are you saying that someone stole your car with the intent of running Matt down, then politely returned it?"

"After he or she wiped the blood off."

Kurt shook his head. "Sorry, that sounds just a little far out for me."

"Personally, I think it's insane. But I don't have any other explanation. Do you?"

She could tell he was thinking very hard. The muscle on the right side of his temple pulsed.

"Well, at least you can eliminate anyone who was at the party," he said finally.

"Not really," she whispered, her throat rough with tension. "A lot of people were at the party, but they wandered in and out. If someone left for twenty or thirty minutes then came back, nobody would have paid any attention."

"You can't be serious!"

"Why not? Even twenty minutes is enough time to drive to my house, get my car, drive back to the Wobbly Barn and waste Matt, then return the car and make an appearance at the Wobbly Barn just before the police arrived."

He studied her expression, as if still unsure of her sanity. "Have you shown your car to the police?"

"No."

"Why not?"

"Would you?"

Kurt blinked frosty blue eyes at her. "You mean they'll either ignore you or figure you were somehow involved, since it was your car?"

"Right. So I have to find some solid proof—something that points to the real driver—before I can go back to them."

"I see." Kurt paused for a moment, glanced away, then turned back and reached out to take her hand. "At least I'm glad that you trust me," he said solemnly.

For a second, her heart stopped. Something about the way he'd stretched out his hand toward her brought back Matt's last moments on this earth. He, too, had reached out for her, but his hand had been bloody and shaking. And this scrap of memory jarred another, even more distressing one out of her subconscious. The memory of Matt's last words:

"WATCH OUT . . . FOR KURT!"

106

Karen slowly lifted her gaze to meet Kurt's beautiful eyes, which were already fixed intently on her. Oh God, why hadn't she remembered Matt's warning before? A ripple of panic swelled in her chest.

"You do trust me. Don't you, Karen?" he asked.

"I have to trust someone," she said dully, praying he couldn't guess the awful suspicions warring in her mind.

Unable to meet his eyes any longer, she looked off across the parking lot at the base of Killington Peak. She couldn't stop asking herself questions: How badly had Kurt wanted to win the Mogul Challenge? Or for that matter, how badly had he wanted to steal her away from Matt? Having two boys compete for her might have been a turn-on under other circumstances, but when one of them ended up with his guts smeared across the road—well, that was carrying things a bit too far.

The question now was—what should she do about Kurt? Get as far away from him as possible, quickly, then call Lieutenant Mancini to tell him about Matt's warning? Or stay close to Kurt and keep an eye on him, hoping he'd make some stupid slip that would dump enough evidence in her lap to make everything clear. Karen gently touched the dent on her car's hood.

"Listen," she murmured hastily, "I guess you're right—I get sort of crazy wanting to find out who did this to Matt." She flashed a plastic smile up at Kurt that would have done a Fifth Avenue mannequin proud. "Want to come back to my house? I make a super cup of hot cocoa."

Dr. Henderson's patients entered his basement office through a private door on ground level at the back of the house, and the gravel driveway had been widened to allow four or five cars to park conveniently near the entryway. When Karen pulled into the drive with Kurt's MG close behind, one other car was parked beside her father's boxy imported sedan.

"We'd better go in through the kitchen. My father is with a patient," she told Kurt.

They climbed the narrow wooden stairs to the main level.

"Looks like you've had a lot of work done on the house," Kurt commented as she fit her key into the lock and swung open the door.

"My parents hired a contractor to modernize the plumbing and wiring and build the office in the basement level."

Karen pulled off her wool cap and gloves, expecting to find the room toasty warm. Instead, a chilly breeze wafted across the kitchen, ruffling her hair. Surprised, she looked around, searching for the source of the draft.

"What's wrong?" Kurt asked.

"I . . . I don't know. Mom? Mom, are you home?" Karen called out before glancing at the calendar on the fridge. "I forgot. Today is her bread-baking class."

Kurt shut the door behind them, and the stream of freezing air stopped. But the house still felt surprisingly cold.

"The furnace must have gone out," Kurt suggested. "Want me to check it?"

Karen shook her head. "If it was the furnace, my father's office would be cold, too. He'd have noticed and done something about it. A window . . ." she murmured, still perplexed.

"I'll check this floor and you—"

But a wave of dread was already flowing through

108

Karen's nerves. She launched herself through the kitchen door toward the hallway stairs that swept up to the second floor.

Karen reached the second floor and ran down the hall past her parents' room straight into her own bedroom. For a long moment, she couldn't quite comprehend what she saw.

"Your room!" Kurt gasped, arriving close behind her. "Who would do this?"

Her beautiful, bright, lacy, white-and-yellow flowered bedroom had been destroyed. Pillows and bedspread were flung on the floor. Her stuffed animals were scattered haphazardly on the carpet, many without their heads which had been torn off and tossed in a different direction. Perfume bottles, jewelry box, lamps, books, papers—the remains of which were strewn across the floor—had been swept off of her bureau and desk top.

However, Karen wasn't concerned with the general chaos in her room. As soon as she'd stepped through the door, her eyes had flown to Romeo's cage. Romeo's *empty* cage!

The silver metal door was open. No twitters or cheeps brightened the silent room. And, on the other side of the stretch of destruction, her bedroom window was flung wide open, a cold wind puffing out the sheer, ruffled curtains.

Burning tears welled up in Karen's eyes and filled her throat. She choked them back as she staggered across the room.

"Romeo!" she cried out the window, the frigid air threatening to freeze her tears as they fell. "Romeo . . ." she sobbed again and again when no little bird flew to her outstretched finger.

Finally, Kurt pulled her back from the window and

closed it firmly, locking the metal latch on the sash. "Will he come to you if you call him?"

"Yes," she sniffled, "if he can."

"Good. Let's check the room first. When I was little, my mother used to keep canaries. If they escaped from their cage, they sometimes flew around until they smacked into a wall and fell down behind a bookshelf or something. Just stunned I suppose."

Karen stooped to check beneath her bed and then, with Kurt's help, proceeded to search hurriedly behind every piece of furniture in the room. However, as she'd feared, they found nothing.

"If he got outside, he couldn't survive for long in this cold!" she cried. "Parakeets are tropical birds."

Kurt nodded grimly. "There's still a chance of finding him. Come on. Keep calling his name. Romeo, right?"

"Yes."

It was already growing dark. Kurt followed her across the snow that lay old and graying across her backyard. They peered up into the treetops, calling out Romeo's name, trudging through knee-deep drifts.

At last, Kurt put his arm around Karen's shoulders and gave her a consoling squeeze. "I don't see him. Sorry."

Karen nodded numbly and turned back with Kurt toward the house. Just before they reached the doorstep, she glimpsed a flash of blue against the dingy snow, and her heart leaped inside her chest. She broke free of Kurt's sheltering arm and bolted for the nearby bush.

Falling to her knees in the snow, she searched among the bare branches for the familiar blue of Romeo's belly feathers. She carefully parted the icy twigs

110

with her trembling fingers, calling his name softly so as not to frighten him.

However, the little bird wasn't perched on a low limb as she'd imagined.

"Oh, no . . ." Karen breathed when she finally spotted him. His unmoving body rested on a pillow of snow beneath the bush. With a sharp pang of grief, she realized that it must have been the branches, not his feathers, that had moved in the wind, revealing him for an instant.

Tenderly, Karen scooped up his tiny body, cradling it to her cheek.

The figure stood in the shadow of the big old house that belonged to the Henderson family. Neither Karen nor Kurt noticed him. She was too busy mourning her dead pet; he was too occupied comforting her and trying to usher her back inside, out of the freezing air.

He'd followed Karen for several days, ever since she resurfaced after Matt's death. But even before that, while she was shut away, he'd kept watch over the house. Somehow, he had to find out how much she knew, or guessed.

As far as he'd been able to discover, Karen had been the only witness to the accident, the last one to speak to Matt before he died. He suspected Matt had discovered his secret and confided in her. But if he had told her anything, she seemed to be keeping the information to herself, possibly until she verified it.

Unfortunately, it was only a matter of time before her snooping around, dropping in on the police, and badgering people to question Matt's death would produce the truth. If a dead pet didn't work, he wondered what he'd need to do to silence her.

* * *

Karen didn't understand why—but Romeo's death affected her every bit as strongly as Matt's had. Only this time she felt better able to handle the pain, and even more determined to discover who had so cruelly killed something she'd loved.

She stomped upstairs to her bedroom and sat down on her bed with Romeo still cushioned in her palms.

"I'll help you bury him if you like," a voice said softly.

Karen looked up, still lost in a red haze of hatred. "What?" she bit off.

"Your parakeet. I'll help you bury him," Kurt repeated.

"No. That can wait."

She looked around at the shambles of her bedroom.

"You should report this to the police," Kurt pointed out solemnly.

"I know. I will . . . but not yet. I still need more information."

"Like what?"

"Like about all of Matt's friends. Whoever did this must know that I don't believe his death was a hit-and-run. I think they want me to stop asking questions."

"I'm glad I was with you. . . . So now you can't suspect me," Kurt said.

Karen gave him a cautious smile. "That's right. You were with me the whole time." *However, you might have been keeping me out of the house long enough for someone else to trash my room and let my bird out!* She studied him briefly, then said, "Tell me about Matt's friends."

Kurt sat down on the bed beside her. "Nona, Brandon, and I were always closest to him."

"But Nona and Brandon knew him longer?"

Kurt nodded. "Nona and Brandon moved in with their aunt when they were very young."

"Their aunt? I thought Mrs. Stewart was their mother and they'd been raised in this area."

"No. They're from somewhere near Boston, I think." Kurt frowned in concentration. "If I remember correctly, their parents were killed in an accident, and their aunt adopted them. Nona was just a baby, and Brandon hadn't started school yet. She had their names legally changed to hers."

"And when did you come to Killington?" Karen asked.

"I came to live with my father after my mother died six years ago. Heinz was involved in several land development projects in central Vermont."

"You don't get along well with him," Karen remarked, remembering the scene at the cafeteria.

"We just don't see eye to eye about some things, I guess." Kurt glanced away from her.

"What about other people who Matt was friendly with, or even just knew casually?"

"Well, that could be anyone at school. I heard that he used to hang out with Frank Roselli in elementary school. I can't see that they had much in common later on, but when you're a little kid anyone who happens to live near you is your buddy."

"What do you know about Frank?" she asked.

"That he drives too fast, and he works his ass off."

"And he steals someone's wheels now and then if he has to deliver a pizza and his own car doesn't start," she added.

"Yeah," Kurt admitted, slowly. "But I don't think Frank would ever—"

"I think he likes Nona, a lot," Karen interrupted. She scrunched up her forehead in concentration. "Matt and Nona never had anything going romantically speaking, did they?''

"Hell, no!" Kurt laughed. "Matt considered Nona sort of a sister, the same way I do. Both of us knew that no one could ever measure up to Brandon in her eyes. She idolizes her brother.''

"I've noticed," Karen said thoughtfully. But that line of thought didn't lead her anywhere for the moment, and she forced herself onward. "What about Jerrie Tilden? Matt used to date her.''

"Sure. Like everyone else. It didn't last.''

"You lasted longer than most boys did with Jerrie," Karen put in before she'd considered the impact of her words. "Sorry," she added when Kurt's face fell.

"It's all right. Jerrie was a mistake. I thought she'd be different with me. That's probably what every guy figures when he falls for her.''

"I think she still likes you," Karen stated reluctantly.

Kurt shook his head. "I know her too well now. She's just attracted by the challenge. If we'd stayed together for another week, *she* would have ditched me. But because I dropped her first, she's chasing me.''

"So there's no reason she'd want to do Matt any harm?''

"None at all. He never even talked about her.''

Karen thought for a minute. "Maybe we're tackling this from the wrong direction.''

"What do you mean?''

"Well, let's assume Matt's death and what happened to my room are somehow connected." She gently laid Romeo on the bedspread beside her. "What do Matt and my room have in common?''

"You," Kurt said bluntly. "So what?''

She stared at him. "You're right. Me." Could it be that someone had killed her boyfriend to get back at her? But she hadn't been in Vermont long enough to make an enemy. Or had she? "Oh," she groaned.

"You thought of someone?"

"Maybe. You know Rosie Geer? She's a sophomore."

Kurt rolled his eyes to the ceiling. "Yeah, she's in my English class. She's little, sort of cute, with brown hair and strange eyes."

"Right. And she despises Nona as well as everyone who hangs out with her. She tried to warn me away from all of you my first day at Killington."

"Why?"

"She said Nona's crowd would use me, then throw me away when they were done. . . . And that Nona and Brandon thought they could run everyone's lives."

Kurt let out a short, sharp laugh. "That's ridiculous!"

"I thought so at the time," Karen murmured. "Did Rosie know Matt very well?"

"Not at all, as far as I know."

"But she knew me," Karen confided. "And I did something that made her very angry." She told him about refusing to steal the pills for her, then catching her trying to borrow her car to visit her college boyfriend. "I forgot to keep my promise and drive her to the Green Mountain campus."

"She sounds weird, but I can't imagine anyone offing your pet bird because you didn't give her a lift." Kurt hesitated. "You know, though, she could have been the one who did this to your room, looking for pills. I mean—" he looked embarrassed "—if you thought you had any here."

"I am on the Pill," Karen admitted, then blushed

115

when Kurt looked interested in the news. "For bad cramps," she added quickly.

"Oh." He coughed and looked flustered for a moment before going on. "So maybe Rosie was up here looking for your prescription, and Romeo escaped by accident."

Karen sighed. "Maybe. But Rosie had a chance to search my room when she was up here before." She got up and checked the drawer of her bedside table, but the slim plastic compact holding her pills was still there. "See?" she said.

Kurt squeezed his eyes shut and rubbed the bridge of his nose. "To be honest, I don't think Matt had any enemies." Then he looked straight at her. "And I can't imagine anyone killing a guy to get back at his girlfriend for being snubbed, no matter how badly the person's feelings might have been hurt."

"I know," Karen admitted. "There's something missing, something I keep trying to remember about that night. I think it's important."

"Maybe it will come back to you," Kurt said, patting her hand.

Karen looked up at him questioningly. *Watch out for Kurt.* Matt's dying warning rumbled through her mind again.

"Maybe it will," she murmured.

Chapter 8

The telephone was ringing as Kurt came through the front door of the condo where he lived with his father. He automatically dove for the receiver.

"Kurt, is that you?" The voice sounded only vaguely familiar at first—then it hit him with the power of a fist coming out of nowhere, burying in his gut, knocking the wind out of him.

"Hi, Mrs. Welch," he whispered.

He hadn't seen Matt's mother or spoken with her since the funeral, and on that particular day she hadn't been capable of more than a few words through her tears.

"I'm glad I caught you, Kurt," she said in a soft voice. "I have a small problem. Perhaps you can help me."

"Sure," he said quickly. "Anything. What is it?"

"Matt's coat . . . at least, the coat he was wearing on the night . . . well, you understand. . . ." Her voice dropped off.

"I'm sorry, I don't understand," Kurt said, wishing he could make this easier for her.

Mrs. Welch cleared her throat. "When the hospital

released Matt's body to the funeral home, they gave us a bag with his belongings in it. His watch, wallet, jacket, and such. I couldn't bear to look at them—not then. But now I'm forcing myself to sort through the things in his room. I was thinking that his younger cousins might enjoy having some of his books and old model airplanes and video games—"

"Of course," Kurt mumbled, feeling his throat close up with emotion. He'd spent whole days cloistered with Matt in his bedroom where they'd hooked up a Nintendo unit to a second-hand TV.

"Anyway," Mrs. Welch continued, "I remembered that we'd left the bag with his things in the car trunk. So I went out to get it. I intended to give the parka to the Salvation Army, if it wasn't in too bad condition."

"That's nice," Kurt mumbled, not knowing what else to say.

"But when I took the parka out of the bag I realized it wasn't Matt's after all."

"What?"

"Matt must have borrowed someone's coat the night of the accident," Mrs. Welch said, sounding distressed. "Well, I just wouldn't feel right throwing it out or giving it away. Unfortunately, there's no name inside. But maybe you'd recognize it. It probably belongs to someone who was at the party, and I'd like to return it. Would you stop by and take a look at it?"

Kurt chewed his bottom lip thoughtfully. The last thing in the world he wanted to do right now was examine the blood-stained clothes his best friend had worn on the night he died.

"Kurt?" Mrs. Welch asked, sounding shaky.

"Sure," he agreed with reluctance. "I'll be right over."

He hung up, but his right hand lingered on the receiver as he mulled over this new development. He was just about to pick up the phone again and call Karen when he sensed someone in the room with him. Tensing, he turned around.

"Who was that on the telephone, Kurt?" Heinz Haller asked pleasantly.

"Mrs. Welch . . . Matt's mother."

His father nodded his white head, his eyes wide and full of understanding for a fellow parent. "How is the poor woman doing?"

"As well as can be expected, I guess," Kurt muttered. He wondered how long his father had been standing there and how much he'd heard. Not that it made any difference—he just didn't like people listening in on his private conversations. He decided against calling Karen for the moment. "I'm going out for a while," Kurt announced, trying to keep his annoyance out of his voice.

"You just got home," Heinz complained. "I thought we might have supper together tonight. We could use some time to talk."

"I . . . I don't think so," Kurt said, feeling guilty for turning his father down even as he dashed out the door.

Someday he supposed he'd have to confront his father and get to the root of their antagonism. But he knew he couldn't handle that now.

Ten minutes later, Kurt knocked on the Henderson's kitchen door. A pretty blond woman with Karen's eyes and a ready smile answered. Kurt had met her once before when he'd come to the house several days after Matt's death. He'd visited, hoping Karen might answer his questions about that night. But neither in her stupor nor, later, in wakefulness had she been able to satisfy

119

his need to know why his friend had died.

"Is Karen home?" he asked.

"Yes, she is," Mrs. Henderson said. "Come in, Kurt."

Kurt stepped into the warm kitchen, which was full of the aroma of apples and cinnamon. Two golden-brown pies sat on the oven top, cooling. Karen had complained about her mother's comical attempts at baking, but from what he could see it looked as if she was improving by leaps and bounds. His stomach rumbled softly.

Opening the hallway door, Mrs. Henderson called up the stairs to the second floor. A moment later Karen appeared, looking out of breath, and he realized she must have been working like crazy to put her room back in order before her parents discovered what had happened.

"Want to go for a ride?" Kurt asked, sending her an urgent message with his eyes.

Karen stared at him for a moment, puzzled, then seemed to understand that he needed to talk to her away from the house. "Sure. I've finished most of my homework."

They said a hasty good-bye to her mother, ran down the back stairs, and climbed into Kurt's car.

"What's up?" Karen asked immediately.

He told her about the coat and watched as a look of satisfaction spread across her face.

"That's it! I knew there was something important about that night that I wasn't remembering clearly. Matt was half-drunk, and he had trouble finding his coat on the rack. I noticed that the one he put on looked too short in the sleeves for him. He must have taken the wrong jacket." Karen gave Kurt a congratulatory pat on the arm.

Suddenly, Kurt was keenly aware of how small his MG was with Karen sitting in the cozy bucket seat beside him. *If I wanted to, I could reach over and touch her, too,* he thought. The image of his hand stroking her silky blond hair then drifting down to gently caress her shoulders was unbelievably tempting.

For days before and since Matt's death he'd tortured himself thinking about Karen. Every time her pretty amber eyes or gorgeous smile or spunky New York accent brought a warm glow to his insides, he felt guilty as hell—because she'd been Matt's girl. But he couldn't help being attracted to her and thinking that if he hadn't been such a jerk, if he'd shown her how much he liked her and refused to back down when Matt started making male animal claims on her, she might be his now.

He kept his hands to himself all the way to Matt's house—although the effort was exhausting.

Matt's mother met them at the front door. "Thank you for coming, Kurt. Oh, Karen!" She looked surprised to see her son's girlfriend, and moisture glazed her eyes. "How are you, dear?" She gave her a warm hug.

"Fine, Mrs. Welch," Karen said. "Kurt told me you had a coat you wanted us to look at."

"Yes." Mrs. Welch pointed at a brown paper grocery bag sitting on the floor by the door. She didn't touch it.

Kurt picked up the bag and peered inside. A popular style tan winter coat with plaid flannel lining was rolled up inside. Even though the coat was inside the bag he could see that the fabric was splotched with dark stains. Not wanting to pull it out in front of Matt's mother and Karen, he hunted around for the label and, finding it, studied the place of manufacture.

Kurt's pulse quickened, and his stomach knotted. He could feel the blood rush out of his face. With clammy hands, he closed the bag.

"I think I know its owner," he mumbled thickly. "I'll return it to him." He started backing toward the door.

"Oh, thank you so much," Mrs. Welch said, apparently glad the matter was now out of her hands.

Karen frowned at Kurt as they climbed back into his car. "What's wrong? Whose is it?"

He looked at her, wondering how she'd take the news—and if this ruined his chances of ever getting together with her romantically. He couldn't make himself come straight to the point. "While we were inside, I was thinking that whoever owns this coat might have been the target of Matt's killer."

"You mean Matt was killed by accident? The driver of the car mistook him for someone else?" Karen looked stunned by the possibility, then her amber eyes cleared slowly. "That makes perfect sense, though. It was snowing so hard I could hardly see four or five feet in front of me. Matt was an average build, and he'd turned his coat collar up, so you couldn't really see much of his face. The driver could probably see even less."

"Add to those factors that it was dark, and Matt was crossing a road he wouldn't be expected to be crossing at that time of night. . . ." Kurt thought out loud.

"Whose coat is it?" Karen asked.

For what seemed to him like a very long time, Kurt was unable to speak. He pulled the coat partially out of the bag, up to its shoulders, and turned the label out for Karen to see.

"Bern, Suisse," she read.

"It was made in Switzerland. It belongs to my father," he told her.

Nona, Jerrie, and Brandon sat at a long wooden table in front of the windows overlooking the Snowshed novice slope. Jerrie and Brandon had just finished giving their last lesson of the day, and they were all three sharing a pizza in the snackbar. It wasn't nearly as good as those Frank Roselli delivered from Pizza Attack, but it was cheap and convenient.

Nona didn't feel much like eating. Her eyes drifted across the crowded snackbar, at last coming back to focus on Jerrie. She was undoubtedly the most striking girl she'd ever known. *But she's empty*, she thought. *She doesn't have a soul.*

Brandon looked across the table at his sister and wiped his mouth with a napkin. His handsome red hair and the little-boy gleam in his eyes seized her by the heartstrings. Their eyes locked, and she smiled at him, feeling almost overcome with devotion.

"Have you seen Karen today?" she asked him.

"Kurt was giving her some pointers on one of the beginner slopes," he said around a mouthful of pizza. "They left at about the same time. Around five, I think."

"Oh."

"I can't stand that girl," Jerrie grumbled.

"Who? Karen?" Brandon asked, sounding surprised.

"She's such a ridiculous flirt. Have you seen the way she's been throwing herself at Kurt lately?"

Nona nearly choked on the nibble of pizza she'd been tossing around in her mouth. Coming from Jerrie that accusation was worse than the pot calling the kettle black. "I don't think Karen has much to do with it.

Kurt told me he's liked her since the first day she arrived."

Jerrie wrinkled her nose. "I don't believe that. I think she's trying to seduce him the same way she seduced Matt. Matt and I were going to get back together, you know."

Nona raised a brow. "No. I didn't know."

"It's true," Jerrie said with a long sigh, studying her perfect red-polished fingernails in the fading sunlight. She could give five hours of strenuous lessons and never chip one. "I think he was in love with me."

Brandon rolled his eyes as if to say, *Give me a break!*

"That's truly tragic," Nona commented.

"And now, as soon as Kurt starts showing an interest in me again, *she* throws herself at him."

"Jerrie," Nona said patiently, "don't you think you've got this all backwards?"

"Huh?" The raven-haired ski instructor looked genuinely puzzled.

"She means," Brandon explained, sounding bored, "you were through with Matt until Karen came along. Suddenly he began to look attractive to you, because you knew you couldn't sink your claws into him. Face it, Jerrie, you're warped."

Jerrie's mouth dropped open, and her cheeks flushed pink. "You make it sound like I'm some kind of nympho or something!"

Brandon winked at Nona. "If the shoe fits . . ."

Jerrie pouted. "Well, at least I don't have to worry about dates. Some people I know rarely go anywhere unless accompanied by their brother."

Nona stiffened. "What's that supposed to mean?"

"Nothing much. Just that I don't have to rely on my family for . . . recreation."

Brandon must have finally caught her drift. He shot to his feet, his face red and twitching. "You bitch! I wouldn't mess around with my sister."

Nona glared at her. "There's nothing wrong with my relationship with my brother. We're just close, that's all."

Jerrie smiled sweetly.

Bending over, Brandon brought his face down on a level with hers. "You don't understand the meaning of the word loyalty, Jerrie. Nona is loyal to me. She'll always be there when I need her, and I'll stand by her. You're just jealous because you don't have anyone like that in your life."

"I will. Just watch me," Jerrie hissed, thrusting her nose in the air. "I'll get Kurt back from that New York tramp, and I'll keep him. You'll see."

Nona laughed. "And how are you going to do that?"

Jerrie opened her mouth in a nasty snarl, then tightened her lips again, a sly expression falling over her eyes. "I have my ways," she said noncommittally.

Karen couldn't sleep that night. At first it was because she kept thinking about Kurt and his poor father. When Kurt had left her that afternoon he'd been in a frenzy. At first he'd begged her to go with him to the police to ask for protection for Heinz, then—for no reason she could understand—he'd changed his mind and asked her not to say anything to anyone until he could find out something more about why anyone would want to kill his father.

"He's always been a mystery to me," Kurt told her as they stood on the landing outside her kitchen door. "I've always held this unexplainable grudge against him, but I can't go on feeling like this forever without being sure why. I'll keep watch over him so that no one gets another shot at him. In the meantime we can look for some answers.''

"Right," she agreed.

But throughout the early hours of the night she'd lain awake, trying to piece together the few clues she now had. As she stared at the ceiling, a strange noise crept over her thoughts.

Reluctantly, she crawled out from under the warm covers and tiptoed across the cold floor to her window. Karen could feel the frosty air penetrating the glass. She pressed her face close to it and peered out into the black night. Almost at once, she was filled with a sense of something evil lingering, waiting just outside her window. Yet there seemed to be no one in sight.

As if drawn to it, her right hand reached to touch the opal necklace where it should have been resting between her breasts—then she remembered having removed it when she undressed for bed. Karen ran to her dresser, lifted the top of her jewelry box, and took it out.

The glass globe was cool to her touch, yet when she opened her fingers after holding it for only a few seconds, it glowed a vibrant, bloody red. The explanation of her body's warmth altering the stones no longer made sense. *She hadn't worn the necklace for hours!*

With shaky fingers, she slowly lifted the necklace and clasped it around her throat, for the first time truly beginning to believe in the power of Nana Gee's opals, but still unsure how to use them.

Someone is out there, she thought, *watching my window*. She felt as if she needed every bit of help she could get now—real or supernatural. Karen closed her eyes and tried to think over the nervous pounding

126

in her head, still cradling the glass globe in her palm.

Common sense told her she should call the police despite her promise to Kurt. She had drawn a number of conclusions by now, too troubling to ignore: Her car had hit and killed Matt Welch, although the driver had intended to plow down the actual owner of the coat Matt had worn—Heinz Haller. Of lesser importance to the police, her room had been demolished and her pet parakeet allowed to freeze to death in an attempt to discourage her from asking too many questions. Sadly, both of these developments were no more than assumptions. No definitive evidence existed to show that her theories were true.

Karen crawled back into her bed and rested against her pillow, listening to the world outside of her room— for a moment, then for a longer time, perhaps for hours. The wind whistled through the tall pine boughs above the old house. Somewhere nearby, branches scraped shrilly against a window.

Think. Think, damn you! Karen ordered herself as dawn edged its way up through the trees in weak pink streaks.

Slowly she reached for the telephone receiver as a plan began to form in her mind. She punched Nona's number by memory. "I want to have a party," she said.

"Huh?" A sleepy voice came over the line. "Hey, do you know what time it is?"

Karen shot a disinterested look at her clock. "Seven-thirty."

"It's Saturday for crying out loud!" groaned Nona.

"Good. Saturday parties are the best."

Silence from the other end.

At last Nona asked, "Are you sure you're ready for

this, Karen? I mean, it's been less than a month since Matt—"

"I know!" Karen interrupted before she could lose her nerve. "But I have to get over this sometime."

"I guess I understand how you must feel," Nona said slowly. "We can have it at my house if you like."

"No. I want everyone to come to the Wobbly Barn."

"You're sure? That won't depress you?"

"I think bringing everyone back together will cheer me up," Karen said emphatically. "Only this party won't be open to the public. I'll just invite a few special people. Can you and Brandon come?"

"I can," Nona said, then hesitated. "Brandon probably has to work tonight. Saturdays are bouncers' busiest nights."

"Too bad." Karen sighed.

"Maybe he can get someone to cover for him for part of the night. I'll ask."

"Thanks." Karen hung up, her head buzzing from lack of sleep but feeling, strangely, clearer than it had in days.

For the next five minutes she scribbled a list of names on a sheet of paper, adding to it and deleting until she was satisfied. She leaned back on her bed and read them over one last time. A surge of confidence washed over her, but out of the corners of her eyes she caught a glimpse of the opals resting on the front of her flannel nightgown. They resembled hot coals in a barbecue, glowing red, a cloud of steam hovering around them in their glass cage.

Is the evil that near, Nana? she asked silently. *Or is the evil right here, inside your necklace?*

For the first time, it occurred to her that she'd never worn the piece of jewelry until she'd come to Vermont.

All the bad things had begun happening then. Karen considered removing the necklace again, but she remembered her grandmother's expression on the day she'd given it to her, her dying eyes full of love and frank concern for her granddaughter's welfare.

"She believed it was good and would protect me," Karen murmured. The stones shot out a pale blue spark, as if to reaffirm her words, then returned to their seething crimson glow.

Karen kept the necklace on.

She had arranged large floor cushions in a semicircle around the hearth of the Wobbly Barn party room, lit the fire, and prepared refreshments before the others arrived. Now all of her guests were seated as orange flames licked their way around the pile of logs and kindling.

Satisfied that the fire wouldn't go out, Karen passed out mugs of hot spiced cider, then took her own place.

"Well, are we all here?" Nona asked, looking interested in what was going on.

"Who cares if we're all here!" Brandon grumbled, moodily. "I have to get back to work. Look, Karen, this obviously isn't a party, so what's up?"

"Nothing's up," she said innocently, taking a sip of her cider. "I just thought it would be nice if we all got together again."

Frank Roselli glanced anxiously at his watch. "I agree with Brandon. This isn't a good time for a party, big or little. I've got a stack of pizzas ready for delivery back at the restaurant. If you have something to say, you'd better say it because I'm leaving in ten minutes, tops."

"That's not very polite," Rosie scolded.

Brandon shot her a wilting glare. "Tough!" he

barked. "Roselli's right. Look, we all miss Matt. So maybe that's what this is all about—saying good-bye to him. Okay, I can dig that. So, let's all say how much we miss him—" Brandon's voice cracked with emotion, "—and then we gotta get going. . . . We have our own lives to live!"

Nora stared at her brother with pain-filled eyes, and Karen almost felt sorry she'd made them come. But she knew that this meeting was necessary. As she glanced around the room at each of their faces, she thought that only Jerrie seemed oblivious to the crushing sense of loss that hovered around them.

Mostly that was because she was too busy trying to catch Kurt's attention with her luminous lavender eyes. Jerrie reached over and squeezed his thigh between two fingers, then giggled softly at his startled expression.

If she touches him one more time, Karen vowed, *I'll kill her!*

Kill? No, not kill. She fervently took back her wish. Even Jerrie didn't deserve death. Matt's accident was enough; she didn't want anyone else to die.

"Are we going to play some music?" Jerrie asked. She fluttered her eyelashes at Kurt. "I'd love to dance."

"Vertically or horizontally?" Rosie asked under her breath.

Unfortunately, Jerrie heard her. "You little bitch!" she shrieked, struggling to get to her feet.

Kurt pulled her back down on her cushion.

"Now, children," Nona chided, "let's not fight." She turned to Karen. "I think you'd better get on with whatever you intend to say before someone yanks someone else's hair out by the roots."

Karen nodded. "I want to tell you a story," she

said quickly. "It's about Matt, in a way, but it has much more to do with someone else."

The room grew silent. Out in the main lounge the band stopped playing, taking their break. All Karen could hear behind her own voice was the wind outside, whipping icily down the mountainside. It seemed to have picked up considerably since sundown.

"The day of the Mogul Challenge trials was supposed to be special to someone," she continued in an even tone. "That was the night this person had planned to kill Kurt's father."

Nona frowned. "Karen, you've been under a lot of stress." She stood up and looked around at the others. "I don't think we should encourage her by listening to this."

"Sit down, Nona," Kurt advised.

Brandon glared at his friend. "If my sister wants to go, she can. Leave her alone."

"I think she should stay," Kurt said. He sounded calm, although Karen knew he was not. "What Karen has to say is true. At least I believe she knows more about Matt's death than the police do. And if my father is involved, I want to know how."

Karen felt all eyes turn to her expectantly. "I don't know everything yet," she admitted. "But I have uncovered several facts."

"So, let's have them," Brandon griped, always impatient.

Karen began again. "Matt was acting strangely on the night of the Mogul Madness party. He seemed distracted, as if he had something very important on his mind. A couple hours into the party, he told me he had to leave for a little while but said he'd be right back. I offered to go with him. He wouldn't let me, but—"

"But you followed him anyway," Jerrie finished for her. "I saw you."

"Yes," Karen continued slowly, making a point of remembering that Jerrie had been watching her. "He was heading across the street, even though his car was in the parking lot here at the restaurant. But I never caught up with Matt. A car was waiting just down the road from the Wobbly Barn, its engine running. As soon as Matt stepped into the road, it started toward him."

"Did you get the license plate number?" Nona asked solemnly.

"No, I didn't then. But I have the number now."

"That's great!" Rosie exclaimed. "All the police have to do is call it in and a computer at the Motor Vehicle Administration will tell them who registered the car."

"The car is mine," Karen said.

A noticeable coolness descended on the room, as if someone had opened a door letting in a draft.

"You're not serious," Nona murmured.

"Someone broke into my parents' garage, took my car, and was sitting in it on the Access Road. Unfortunately for that person, when Matt left the Wobbly Barn he picked up the wrong coat, one belonging to Kurt's father, and he appeared at about the time Mr. Haller usually left the Wobbly Barn. Heinz Haller was the intended victim, you see."

"The driver never knew it was Matt?" Frank whispered hoarsely.

"Right. Whoever was behind the wheel left him for dead, believing they'd run down the right person. Then they drove just far enough down the road to clean off the front of my car before returning it to the garage."

"Then it couldn't have been a tourist," Jerrie said

with surprising clarity, given her distraction in Kurt's presence.

"No. Not a tourist. It had to be someone who knew me, but most importantly, someone who also held a terrible grudge against Mr. Haller and had studied his habits. The killer was counting on the fact that Kurt's father routinely crossed the street to the Wobbly Barn after a day of work at his office then returned home between ten and eleven P.M."

"Heinz is pretty predictable," Kurt seconded. "He stays at the Barn for about three hours every night, having dinner, chatting with the manager and a few older locals who hang out in the bar."

"There were a couple other clues," Karen continued. "Matt whispered something to me just before he died." She paused to look around the circle of faces. "He said: 'Watch out for Kurt.'"

Kurt stared at her, and she could see the muscles in his neck knot with tension. "That's impossible," he choked out.

Karen took a deep breath, knowing she was taking a risk—one that might jeopardize her life if she wasn't careful. "I know," she said slowly, meeting Kurt's troubled blue eyes. "And at first I must have blanked out Matt's last words, because they didn't make sense. When I finally remembered what he'd said, I took it literally, as a warning. I was afraid to be alone with you, Kurt."

He shook his head sadly. "Why would Matt say something like that? He couldn't have been intentionally trying to mislead you—he was dying for crying out loud!"

"No, he wasn't trying to mislead me . . . or warn me. I was his girlfriend, but we'd really only known each other for a month. We were never that close—

not like you and he had become. He was afraid *for* you, not *of* you, because he'd discovered the truth. He had discovered a secret about your father, or possibly about your family, and he knew something dangerous was brewing—what it was, he wasn't sure. But if it had anything to do with revenge, he feared for your life."

Karen leaned forward and put her cup of cider on the floor beside her. "The night of the party, he left to find your father . . . to warn him that he was in danger. Because he'd been drinking, Matt probably lost track of time and didn't realize Heinz might still be in the bar—where he actually was."

Rosie rocked forward suddenly onto her knees. "Oh, geez! Then Matt wasn't warning you, he was asking you to *protect* Kurt!"

No one said a thing for several minutes. Kurt's face was as white as the ashes gathering on the floor of the fireplace. Jerrie stared morosely at her long painted fingernails. Rosie looked as if she was about to start crying.

At last, Brandon shot to his feet. "This is ridiculous. Assassinations. Warnings of doom! Look, I loved Matt, too. But I'm not going to invent wild tales to explain a drunk driver mowing him down. It just happened! For God's sake, forget it!"

He bolted for the door. Nona jumped up to follow him, but Frank seized her arm.

"No. Let him go. He'll cool down better on his own," he said gently.

Nona was visibly shaken as she faced Karen. "I thought you were our friend. Why are you doing this?"

"Because we have to reach the truth, one way or another," she said solemnly.

"Why don't you go to the police and see what they think of all this?" Frank asked.

"I know why," Jerrie said nastily before Karen could answer. "Because they'll laugh in her face. What sort of black spot is there on Kurt's family? Why would anyone want to kill Mr. Haller? Was he a spy or something? The last of the Nazis to escape Germany?"

Nona shook her head. "Karen, I have to agree with Brandon and Jerrie. Your imagination is totally off the wall, whether you'll admit it or not."

Karen looked at each of them, needing to get one last message across to the right person. "I'm sorry you don't believe me, but I'm going to find out why Matt died," she promised. "Nobody is going to stop me."

Karen sat alone in front of the fireplace. The others had left, and a bad blizzard was obviously brewing. The wind howled and whistled around the splintered barn boards.

Karen didn't really want to leave the warm safety of the party room, but she knew she had to. She'd set the stage for a confrontation. Now she had to move on to the next step.

"I came back," a deep voice announced from behind her.

She jumped, afraid for an instant, but calmed as soon as she saw Kurt's face.

"I wasn't sure that you would," she said with a sigh, standing up.

"I had to check on my father. I asked him if he had anything to hide, anything from his past I should know about. But he just made a joke about it, said there was nothing more than a couple of parking tickets to tarnish the Haller name.''

"Is he all right alone?" she asked.

"I made him promise to stay home with the doors locked and not answer for anyone." Kurt took her hands in his and smiled at her warmly. "I'm glad you decided to trust me."

"Me, too." She gave him a tired grin as he pulled her close and hugged her. She snuggled against his shoulder, feeling warm, protected, and even a little . . . loved. For that moment she could believe that everything was going to be all right.

"You threw me when you told everyone about Matt's last words," Kurt whispered. "Did you make it up or was that really what he said?"

"I didn't make it up," she told him sadly. "He must have really cared about you, Kurt."

"Then the least I can do is help find out who's behind this mess. What do we do now?" he asked.

"Nothing. We wait for the killer to make a move. There are five suspects, if we eliminate ourselves, because those five people are the only ones who knew your father's habits well enough *and* knew that I'd arrived early with Nona to decorate, leaving my car available."

Kurt ticked off names on his fingers: "Jerrie, Rosie, Frank, Brandon, and Nona."

Karen looked up at him for a long, tense moment. "Right. One of them killed Matt."

Chapter 9

Kurt had his own key to Brandon's place—or at least it was a key he was free to use—hidden in a small magnetic box that was pushed up into the clothes dryer vent.

He let himself into the apartment over the garage, helped himself to a soda out of the fridge and a handful of potato chips, then settled down on the sofa with a copy of *Skier's Digest*.

The apartment was perfect for a single guy—just two rooms: a combined living room and kitchen, and one bedroom with a bathroom the size of a small closet. The living room was sparsely furnished with a second-hand sofa and armchair with dark green plaid cushions, and a low coffee table. A braided rug, almost identical to one in Mrs. Stewart's parlor, lay on the floor. The cooking area was just a few feet of space at the end of the living room, equipped with a sink, mini-stove, and compact refrigerator.

After only a few minutes, Kurt tossed the magazine onto the coffee table. His eyes had grown so heavy he could hardly keep them open. He looked at his watch. It was almost midnight, but Brandon might not be home for another hour. Usually Kurt crashed on the couch, but he didn't intend to sleep here tonight. He'd just come to kill a little time, to wait until his father fell asleep so he wouldn't have to talk to him about anything too deep tonight. He had too much on his mind. Yet he didn't want to leave Heinz alone in the condo all night either.

Kurt was halfway out the door when he remembered the other skiing magazine he'd loaned Brandon a couple of weeks earlier. A minute of rummaging through newspapers and magazines in a wooden bucket beside the sofa produced nothing. Kurt decided to try the bedroom.

Spotting the bright *Skier's Digest* logo from across the room, Kurt made a hasty grab for it on the bedside stand. A handful of coins flew off the wooden surface, rolling across the floor.

"Damn!" he whispered, dropping to his knees to chase down the dime and nickel he'd seen roll under the table.

The nickel was close to the front, but the dime must have traveled further because, after feeling around, he still couldn't locate it. He reached as far as he could, and the back of his hand rustled against something. Curious, he turned his hand over and ran his fingertips along the underside of the table. A piece of paper seemed to be taped to the wood.

With mixed feelings, Kurt got to his feet and started slowly toward the bedroom door. *Brandon's hiding something*, he mused. *Whatever it is, it's probably none of my business*.

However, what if it had something to do with Heinz? Something to do with Matt's death? He swerved around and made a beeline for the table.

Not wanting to risk tearing the paper before he got

a good look at it, he took everything off the table top, carefully removed the two drawers, then turned the frame upside down and studied its underside.

A thick, yellowed business-size envelope had been fixed to the bottom with masking tape. His hands sweating, he pried off the envelope and opened it.

For a long time, Kurt sat in the middle of the floor, reading, soaking up information. A part of his past slipped into place, and he was filled with horror at the misery that had already taken place and the misery that no doubt was still to come—all because of a long ago skiing vacation.

Karen stood outside the Wobbly Barn, watching Kurt's car disappear into the darkness. He hadn't driven across the street to his condo as she'd expected but down the Access Road, away from the ski slopes. *He must be going to Brandon's*, she thought. Now that Matt was gone, he seemed to spend even more time with the other boy.

As she turned back toward her own car, her glance shifted unintentionally to the strip of pavement directly in front of the Barn—the spot where Matt had died. She fought the aching need to cry. She wouldn't let herself do that. Not now while so much was at stake. Forcing herself to stand outside in the cold, taking long, slow breaths, she finally regained her composure. By the time she climbed into her own car, her nose and ears and fingers were numb and brittle with frost.

Karen drove down the mountain on the Access Road, turning right at the intersection onto Route Four. Heading for her own house, she passed the Stewarts'. Kurt's car was parked out front. The house was dark, but a light was on in the apartment over the garage, and she automatically slowed down.

Just then, the door at the top of the wooden staircase flew open, and Kurt appeared, his face a mask of strain in the dim yellow porch light. One look at his expression and Karen knew something had to be wrong. She pulled over, flung open the car door, and ran to meet him at the bottom of the steps outside the garage.

He looked down at her dully, his mouth a grim line.

"What's that?" she asked, eyeing the crumpled yellow envelope in his right hand.

He bit his lip and blinked, looking dazed.

"Come on," she said, pushing him toward her car, "I'd better drive. You're in no condition to sit behind a wheel."

"What about my car?"

"I'll move it to the other side of the block . . . out of sight. You can ride with me back to my house, and we'll talk there."

Karen's parents had already gone to bed, and she was relieved that she wouldn't have to explain Kurt's late visit. She made instant coffee, spooning plenty of sugar into Kurt's cup without even asking if he took it. *Good for the shock*, she thought vaguely, worried by how pale he looked. She led him into the living room where they sat cross-legged on the carpet, their cups on the coffee table in front of them.

"Drink up. There's more." She couldn't take her eyes off the old envelope he'd clutched all the way back from Brandon's apartment "What's in that?" she asked again after he'd finished a second cup.

He laid the envelope in front of her without a word. Taking this as permission to read its contents, she unclasped the flap with her fingernail and shook out scraps of paper: six newspaper clippings with names highlighted in fluorescent green. As she read the first article clipped from the *International Herald Tribune*, her hands began to shake.

"I could sit here and read all this," she murmured, "but we may be short on time. You'd better give me a quick summary, if you can."

Kurt spoke, his voice hoarse with emotion. "My mother apparently left my father and took me with her following a terrible accident. I was about two years old at the time, and we had been living in Grindelwald in the Swiss Alps. When I was older and I asked about my father, she always told me that he was dead, but she never really explained how he'd died. She once mentioned that he'd made his living by escorting ski tour groups."

Karen nodded, listening intently.

"It seems that one day, after skiing for less than an hour, two members of a party complained of being tired and wanted to return to the lodge. My father took the shortest route back, leading the entire group across a snowfield—a flat area of virgin snow between several peaks. Maybe he was just trying to take it easy on the less experienced skiers. Whatever his reason, the decision was a bad one. Crossing a snowfield is the sort of thing someone who knows the mountains would never do unless he was alone and very careful. A group of ten or so, like that one, trekking across an undisturbed field creates subtle vibrations that might start an avalanche."

Karen's heartbeat quickened. "And that's what happened?"

"Yes. There was an avalanche. Mountains of ice and snow began to fall on them."

"But how does that relate to here and now in Vermont?"

Kurt pointed to news photos taken after the disaster—a little cluster of people huddled in blankets, their expressions bleak and dazed. A younger Heinz Haller was clearly one of them. She read the caption:

SOLE SURVIVORS OF TRAGIC HOLIDAY AVALANCHE.
SIX PERISH BENEATH TONS OF SNOW.

"Only four lived?" she whispered.

Kurt gave a stiff nod. "By the time the ski patrol reached the group, more than half had suffocated or been crushed to death under the ice."

"Oh, God!" Karen gasped. She flipped through the remaining articles, some in German, others torn from the *Tribune*, an English-language newspaper published in Europe. "None of the names sounds familiar," she murmured, "except for your father's. Von Haller. He must have Americanized his name when he came to this country."

Kurt stared at one of the clippings. "Of course, I knew he'd done that because von Haller was my name, too. But a lot of immigrants alter their names, so I didn't think anything of it. I recognize one other name, though. A young married couple that died—Mr. and Mrs. Daniel Curtis."

Karen wrinkled her nose. "Curtis. No, it means nothing to me."

"It wouldn't." Kurt's voice dropped to a shaky whisper. "Curtis was Brandon's and Nona's last name before their aunt and uncle adopted them. Brandon once told me that their aunt legally changed their names because she wanted the two of them to consider her and her husband their parents, to forget the past."

"Apparently Brandon couldn't," Karen murmured.

"Right. He must have recognized my father from

these old clippings. Possibly his aunt had kept them. At any rate, Heinz had money put away and used it to buy up some land and build condos near a couple resort areas in the United States before I came to live with him. He invested wisely. By the time my mother died and he sent for me, he was finishing a fifty-unit project in New Hampshire. I lived with him there. Later we moved here, to Killington. Neither of my parents ever mentioned the accident, but that must have had something to do with why their marriage broke up."

"Your father may have wanted to protect you from the past. That's why he never told you. Or maybe he thought you'd hate him if you found out."

Kurt sighed. "Or leave him, like my mother did. But I think I would have been better off knowing."

"So, it must have been Brandon behind the wheel of my car," Karen murmured. "He killed Matt."

"It looks that way. But if he did it, it wasn't intentional. He wanted to kill my father."

"Any way you cut it, it's still murder," Karen muttered grimly. She looked up into Kurt's pale blue eyes which were so sad now. "Do you think he'll try again?"

Kurt thought for a moment. "I've never known Brandon to give up on anything. If he wants vengeance, he'll get it . . . or die trying."

"I'd better go to the police," Karen said. "Your father needs professional protection."

Kurt stood up. "I'll go with you."

"No. You go home and stay with Heinz until I can get back with the police. He shouldn't be alone as long as Brandon is loose."

Kurt nodded. "Anyway, I guess it's time we had a long talk."

* * *

Nona watched as Brandon screeched out of the parking lot of the nightclub where he worked. She'd rarely seen him as angry as he'd been at the Wobbly Barn earlier that night. Because she'd been worried about him, she'd talked Jerrie into going with her to The Drifts to try to calm him down. But they hadn't succeeded. In fact, her brother's temper had flared out of control, and he'd insulted several customers. Eventually his boss got fed up and sent him home for the night.

"I don't blame poor Brandon at all," Jerrie huffed. "Do you believe the nerve of that Karen? She was accusing one of *us* of killing Matt!"

Nona shrugged. "Ignore her. She isn't thinking straight. I bet she's still in love with Matt. Maybe looking for the reason he died is part of the healing process."

"Healing my ass!" Jerrie fumed. "She's creating a mystery of Matt's death to seduce Kurt."

Nona laughed. "That's ridiculous."

"Oh, yeah? Did you see the way he was looking at her tonight? He couldn't keep his baby blues off her."

"You have a one-track mind, girl," Nona said dryly. "Forget Kurt. There are plenty of other fish in the sea."

"I don't want another fish. I want Kurt!" Jerrie thrust out her lower lip and pouted. In the next second, her lavender eyes sparkled with wicked inspiration in the glow from a nearby street light. "And I'll get him."

"What's that supposed to mean?"

"Nothing," Jerrie murmured. She shifted her glance suddenly.

Nona swiveled around to see what had caught her

attention. Rosie Geer had approached so quietly that neither of them had noticed her standing within hearing range on the other side of Nona's car.

"What do *you* want?" Jerrie snapped.

Rosie opened her mouth, then closed it as if having second thoughts.

"Don't pay any attention to Jerrie," Nona advised. "Her hormones are on the warpath. What is it, Rosie?"

"I . . . I was just wondering if either of you could drop me off at my house. I hitched over here with Frank, but I don't have a ride home."

Jerrie tossed her long black hair over one shoulder. "I'm heading the other way," she said quickly.

"What do you mean? You live practically next door to Reverend Geer," Nona pointed out.

"I can't give her a ride. Okay? So sue me!"

"Why not?"

"I have to meet someone," Jerrie bit off.

Nona squinted suspiciously. "You're going to hassle Karen, aren't you?"

"Hassle is an understatement," Jerrie tossed over her shoulder as she unlocked her car door and climbed in. "I'm going to find a way to get Kurt back."

"What are you going to do?" Nona demanded.

"Whatever it takes!"

Nona let out a weary sigh as Jerrie sped away, leaving the other two girls in the middle of the parking lot. Keeping peace between all of her friends was sure tough on the nerves. Jerrie was totally unpredictable. And she felt responsible for Brandon—these days he seemed to bear watching more than usual. Then there was Karen, who hadn't turned out to be as easygoing a person as she'd at first thought. Even Kurt was making everything more complicated by siding with the

New Yorker. In fact, Brandon was furious with both Kurt and Karen now, but especially with Karen.

Sadly, Nona could foresee a time when her brother might end her friendship with Karen. Blood is thicker than water, he'd always said. A curious expression, she thought, remembering the congealed, semi-frozen dark red pool in the middle of the road where Matt had lain, his life oozing out of him. True, blood was physically thicker. But friends were so hard to keep these days.

Nona felt Rosie staring at her. The minister's daughter gave her the creeps.

She glanced up from the frozen ground. "I suppose you still need a ride?" Nona asked.

Rosie nodded sheepishly.

Nona shrugged. The snow had begun again and was getting heavier. "Why not?" she said.

Frank Roselli hastily popped a couple of slices of pepperoni into his mouth and washed them down with a swig of root beer while jamming a small cheese pizza into an insulated box. He'd been racing all over town for the past six hours and hadn't found time for dinner. He was hungry and tired and thought he'd scream if the phone rang one more time.

The telephone let out a loud jangle just as he dashed for the door.

"I'm going!" he shouted.

He could hear his father taking the call in the kitchen. "Hurry back, Frankie! You got another delivery for the Hawk's Nest!"

"I'm movin' fast as I can!" he called out as the door slammed shut behind him.

Frank carefully placed the pizza on the passenger seat beside him and backed the station wagon around, the tires throwing gravel. However, he patiently allowed two cars to pass by on the Access Road before pulling out. As he drove, he kept an eye on the speedometer.

He hadn't known Matt Welch very well, but his death had made him think twice about taking any more chances on Killington's slick mountain roads. He considered himself lucky the police hadn't stopped him the night of Matt's accident, since he habitually exceeded the speed limit by at least fifteen miles per hour and everyone in town knew it.

Tonight Frank drove at a sensible, and legal, thirty-five toward the Winter Crest condos. Looking down at the receipt taped to the box, he read the name on the order: Heinz Haller.

He couldn't remember ever delivering to Kurt's father, although Kurt himself had called in plenty of orders—most often from Brandon's place. He wondered if Kurt had told his old man Karen's wild theory about Matt's death—that Haller himself had actually been the target. Probably not. Why scare the crap out of the guy for nothing?

He knocked on the condo door and waited, tapping his foot, humming some rap tune he'd heard on the radio on the way over. The door swung open.

Haller was fishing in his wallet for the right combination of bills while he propped open the door with one foot. "You said it was seven dollars on the telephone."

"That's right."

The man's hair was so thin and white, it looked almost nonexistent in the dark. His baldness made his eyes look unusually large, as if he was always staring. If his build had been a little different, he might have appeared frail. But he had the physique of an athlete who'd gone into semiretirement.

"Guess you must be hungry. It's pretty late," Frank commented pleasantly.

Haller looked up, the bills at last selected. "Oh, yes. I decided to stay in tonight, but there really wasn't much in the house that seemed appetizing. Did you have a lot of deliveries to make tonight?"

"No more than usual."

Haller laid eight dollar bills on his palm. "Keep the change, son. I hope you don't drink and drive," he continued, sounding concerned. "I always warn Kurt against such irresponsible behavior."

"I never drink when I'm working," Frank assured him, starting for the door.

Haller stepped in front of him. "That's good. You're a smart boy." He smiled tentatively.

His exit blocked, Frank frowned at Haller, wondering what was on the man's mind. "Is there . . . um . . . anything else I can do for you, sir? I have soda in the car if you like."

"No, thank you." The older man looked thoughtful for a moment, then met Frank's puzzled glance. "I suppose I shouldn't put you in the position of informing on my son. But I couldn't help wondering if you'd run into him tonight."

Frank didn't see how telling the old man that he'd seen Kurt would hurt. "He was at the Wobbly Barn for a little while."

"Was he? That's surprising. He rarely spends any time there . . . or here, for that matter." Haller suddenly looked depressed.

Frank took pity on him and, laughing, slapped him on the back. "Hey, you're not alone, Mr. Haller. My mom's the same way about me. She says she only sees me at home when the restaurant's closed."

The man didn't appear to be cheered. "The pizza will get cold," he mumbled. "I was hoping Kurt and I could have dinner together tonight." His glance dropped sadly to the floor.

Feeling uncomfortable, Frank took advantage of Haller's preoccupation to slip around him and out the door.

Although it was late, Karen managed to track down Lieutenant Mancini by calling a number he'd left with her parents on the chance she might remember more details about Matt's death. He met her at the state police barracks in Rutland.

In his office, he silently studied the newspaper clippings she'd brought him. Then she led him out to the parking lot where, still without comment, he examined the front end of her car under the beam of a strong flashlight. It was all she could do to keep from jumping up and down and squealing with anticipation.

"So you believe that your car was the murder vehicle," he said, at last.

"I'm sure of it," she insisted excitedly. "I remember how the front of the car struck Matt. The dents match and are definitely recent."

Mancini nodded, making a few notes on a yellow legal pad. "We'll have to check this out then."

Karen felt her smile begin to stiffen at the note of skepticism in his voice. "Can't you just go to The Drifts and arrest Brandon right now? Kurt's father is in danger as long as he's free."

The lieutenant looked at her in the dark. "You're assuming a great deal, aren't you?"

"Assuming? You saw those old clippings. Brandon's obsessed with his parents' death and tried to kill

149

Mr. Haller . . . Mr. von Haller. It's pretty obvious that poor Matt was just in the wrong place at the wrong time."

"That's one possibility," Mancini allowed hesitantly, turning toward the barracks.

Karen couldn't believe her ears. She jogged after him. "Listen, whether you believe Brandon is guilty or not, shouldn't you at least bring him in for questioning and give Mr. Haller some protection?"

Mancini held the door open for her. "I'll do my job," he assured her gruffly. "That doesn't include hauling in suspects without substantial evidence."

"But—"

"As for protection, central Vermont isn't what you'd call a hotbed of crime. Most of our arrests are traffic violations—speeding, parking, illegal lane changes. During the high tourist season we get a few pickpockets and an occasional car break-in. There's no budget for round-the-clock bodyguards."

"But . . ."

"It's natural for the boy to be interested in his parents' background and keep a few mementoes." Mancini entered his office and turned on her with a calm but tired smile. "The fact that they died suddenly in a tragic accident is all the more reason he should be curious. Besides, we don't even know that Kurt's father is the von Haller in these clippings."

"Kurt is sure that's him. His own son ought to know!"

"I think you'd better leave this to me," Mancini said in a firm voice. "I'm inclined to agree that the events surrounding the Welch boy's death sound a good deal more complex than we at first suspected. I promise you, I'll be in touch soon."

"Soon?" she gasped. "You're not going to send someone tonight?"

He shook his head. "Go home and get some sleep, Karen. You've done your part."

Hot, angry tears clogged her throat. "You said you wanted to nail the bastard who killed Matt!" she choked out. "You've got your chance now!"

Mancini gave her a long, solemn look. "Karen, I'm more than eager to prosecute any hit-and-run driver to the limit of the law. But I can't drag in the first suspect I come across, then see how much evidence I can scrape together to convict the guy. You've heard of due process of law . . . innocent until proven guilty . . . that sort of thing?"

"Of course," she moaned hopelessly.

"Well, I don't intend to screw up this case. If Brandon Stewart was responsible for Matthew Welch's death, I want to tread carefully from here on. Everything has to be done by the book. I don't want a judge throwing out the evidence on the grounds that it was improperly gathered."

Karen took a deep breath. "You mean the clippings . . . the way we found them."

Mancini nodded. "Any decent defense attorney will claim that Kurt broke into Brandon's apartment and stole those clippings. Technically, he'll be right."

Suddenly, she felt deflated, helpless, and more than a little stupid.

"Listen," he said in a strong but quiet voice, "starting tomorrow I'll assign a couple of men to follow up on those news stories and take a closer look at your car. If possible, you should return the articles to where you found them. I've taken down the names of the newspapers and their dates. And," he added, "get some sleep."

"Get some sleep," Karen muttered in frustration as she climbed the stairs outside her own kitchen twenty minutes later. How could she sleep at a time like this? She hoped Kurt was keeping a close watch on his dad.

Her fingers brushed up against something as they closed around the cold metal handle of the screen door. She looked down, startled to find a slip of paper tucked into the handhold. Pulling the note free, she held it up to the porch light.

KAREN—MEET ME AT BEAR MOUNTAIN BASE LODGE IMMEDIATELY. IMPORTANT!

JERRIE

She frowned at the hand-printed block letters. Did Jerrie know something she hadn't been able to reveal at the Wobbly Barn in front of the others?

It was possible, she supposed. Jerrie might be a tramp, but she wasn't stupid. Karen considered giving Kurt a call to ask if he wanted to go along, but after a moment's thought she decided that wasn't such a hot idea. It was more important that he stay with his father. And, after all, he and Jerrie still weren't on best terms following their breakup. Meeting like this might prove uncomfortable for both of them, and that could dampen Jerrie's willingness to talk to her.

She returned to her car and headed for Bear Mountain.

Chapter 10

Karen stepped out of her car and looked around. Although there were no lights on Bear Mountain, a full silver moon hung over the deserted ski trails, illuminating the mountainside, casting deep shadows behind the gigantic snow moguls on the Outer Limits trail and the surrounding pines. Neither of the two quad chair lifts was moving. No one was in sight.

Only two other cars were parked in the lot near the base lodge. She guessed that they must belong to people who worked nights cleaning the gift shop, locker rooms, and snack bar inside the lodge. Neither one was Jerrie's little foreign roadster; they both appeared to be empty.

The temperature was still dropping, the air growing chillier with each blast of arctic wind. Karen shivered and clapped her gloved hands together, hoping Jerrie would show soon. The light snow that had been swirling about all night began to fall faster. She guessed that within the next hour the blizzard would strike full force.

Without thinking about what she was doing, Karen

153

reached into the neck of her jacket and pulled out the opal necklace.

"Ah!" The exclamation involuntarily escaped her lips, for the little glass bauble felt painfully hot, even through her leather gloves. She dropped the necklace on the outside of her parka to keep it as far away from her skin as possible.

Inside the globe, the opals glowed a fiery, mesmerizing red. Wordlessly—but no less urgently—they cried out a warning to her. *Danger! Danger! Danger! Run! Leave this place!*

Karen could hardly pull her eyes away from them, but she decided that she had to ignore their message, if that was what it was, one last time. If Jerrie's information convinced Mancini she was right about Brandon, the risk would be worth it.

Something moved on the far side of the parking lot.

Karen squinted into the clouds of flakes. Disappearing behind the base lodge was a slim figure in a yellow ski jacket, collar pulled up, knit cap covering the head. She was carrying skis over her shoulder.

"Jerrie!" she called out, breaking into a run.

As she rounded the lodge, she caught sight of the other girl again through the thickening billows of snow. Jerrie approached the loading area of the first quad lift, pausing at a metal box fixed to the side of a small storage shack. The cable that ran from the foot to the summit of the mountain jerked to life in a long fluid line. Jerrie snapped her heels down on her skis and prepared to board the lift.

"Wait!" Karen cried frantically. She bounded across the snow, slipping on icy patches, and, at the last moment, threw herself into the departing bench as it swept up the mountainside.

Karen turned, expecting to see Jerrie at the other

end of the four-passenger seat. Nona was there instead, moving her ski poles out of the way, pulling the lap bar up as they rose at a sharp angle.

"What are *you* doing here?" Karen demanded.

"Saving your life. I had to warn you." Nona drew a jagged breath, coughing when the cold air hit her lungs. "You have to get out of Killington. . . . Go back to New York."

"I'm not leaving," Karen said with determination.

"You have to or——"

"It was Brandon, wasn't it? Brandon was driving my car and killed Matt."

Nona turned her head away so that Karen could no longer read her expression. "No," she whispered hoarsely.

"Denying it won't change the truth," Karen said. "He was trying to kill Heinz Haller, the man responsible for your parents' death."

When Nona at last faced her, tears were shimmering in her eyes. Her lips were ghoulishly purple with cold, and they barely moved when she spoke. "How did you find out?"

Karen thought uneasily about the clippings left unguarded in her car. "Different ways. That's not important. You've got to realize that Brandon needs help. He killed Matt."

"He didn't mean to," Nona argued.

"Whether or not he meant to is beside the point. Murder is murder, he just hit the wrong person."

Nona stared into the swirling snow above the mountainside.

"Look," Karen persisted, "if he turns himself in, a good lawyer might make a case for temporary insanity. The judge could order that he be put in a hospital where he can get help. But if he succeeds in

155

murdering Haller, Brandon will probably spend the rest of his life in prison.''

"No!" Nona bit off. "No one is going to take Brandon away from me.''

Karen's stomach tightened at the resolve in the other girl's voice. "Nona, please be realistic.''

A cold gust hit them as the lift rose above a sheltering bank of pine trees. Karen tucked her head down into the collar of her coat to protect her cheeks. When she looked up again, Nona had turned around and was staring over the back of their chair toward the base of the mountain. Karen followed her gaze. Someone was standing beside a snowmobile, tampering with the quad lift's control box. And she only had to take one look at the adoring expression on Nona's face to figure out who it was.

"What's Brandon doing?''

"Stopping the lift, I guess,'' Nona murmured.

Karen glared at her in shock. "You had this planned all along, didn't you? Somehow you found out about Jerrie's note and decided to take advantage of it.''

"*Jerrie's* note?'' Nona smiled crookedly.

A sickening feeling filled Karen's stomach as she finally realized the seriousness of her own danger. "*You* sent it?''

"Of course. I had to warn you. Now it's too late. Brandon's here—''

The lift jerked to a stop. Karen clutched the safety bar in front of her. A lump of fear swelled in her throat, and she held on as the chair swayed violently in the blustery wind. Looking down past her feet, she could see the rocky crevice at the foot of a cliff known to local skiers as Devil's Drop. The jagged black rocks cast an ugly scar across the gleaming new snow.

When Karen looked up again, Nona was studying

her face intently. Her eyes had grown hard and lusterless in the moonlight. Her mouth formed a tight grimace as she reached toward her. "I'm sorry, Karen. I like you. I really do. I just didn't think you'd become a problem."

Horrified, Karen pulled away. "What the hell are you talking about?" Then Nona's meaning hit her. "That first day we met at school, you were setting me up!"

Nona blinked at her innocently. "We had to use someone's wheels to kill von Haller. Brandon figured it would work better if the car belonged to a tourist. Tourists go barhopping then drive the icy roads too fast. The police are forever pulling them out of snowdrifts. And von Haller crossed the road between the Wobbly and his condos almost every night at the same time."

"But counting on borrowing a tourist's car on short notice wasn't very dependable."

Nona nodded solemnly.

"You even set me up with Matt," Karen murmured, "so you could keep an eye on me. Then the night of the party, you asked me to help with the decorations and insisted on driving to be sure my car would be at home and available for Brandon."

Nona smiled, actually looking pleased. "Right! Everything worked out so well, until . . ."

"Until what?" Karen asked vaguely, distracted by Brandon's movements. He had driven the snowmobile up the steep slope. Standing directly beneath them, he was waving at his sister, as if signaling her to quit gabbing and get on with the execution. Personally, Karen preferred to chat a while longer.

"Until Matt suspected we were planning to harm Haller," said Nona. "Brandon must have had a little too much beer one night and let something slip.''

"Matt saw Brandon leave the party room," Karen guessed. "He decided to warn Haller."

Nona shrugged. "I suppose. At any rate, he was crossing the road at the wrong time. Poor Brandon . . . he didn't mean to kill his best friend."

Poor Brandon? What about poor Matt? Or poor Kurt, whose father was a marked man? Or poor me! a voice screamed inside Karen's head.

"Nona," she choked out, "you and Brandon have to forget the past. Kurt's father never intended to kill your parents or those other people. After the avalanche, he lost his job, his wife and child, and he was forced to leave Europe to start a new life. Isn't that punishment enough?''

"No!" Nona barked, suddenly coming alive again, edging closer to her along the bench.

"What about the note?" Karen gasped, desperate to come up with anything to distract her. "If you kill me, the police will discover it and be suspicious."

"Brandon found it in your car . . . along with the old newspaper clippings you took from his room. That was really stupid, Karen. Once we discovered they were missing, we knew you must have discovered the truth. No . . . your death will be an accident just like Matt's as far as the police are concerned."

Karen cringed as far away from Nona as possible, sensing that at any moment the other girl would lunge at her and try to wrestle her out of the chair lift. "Then how will you arrange a third death—Kurt's father's— without arousing suspicion?"

"Brandon says that shouldn't be hard. Everyone in town knows that he spends plenty of lonely hours at the bar in the Wobbly Barn. His son rejects him, his wife left him years ago, then died. Maybe he's afraid his construction business is going sour what with all the talk of a recession. I'd say he's a pretty depressed individual.''

"Suicide?"

"Of one sort or another. We won't have much trouble arranging a plausible scenario.'' Nona sighed. "Then it will be finished. At last. Right, Bran?'' she whispered affectionately, as if the figure far below could hear.

The wind roughed Brandon's blazing red hair into a devilish mane. He stared up at the two girls, a glaze of madness brightening his green eyes, reminding Karen of a wild creature that knows its prey is, at last, cornered.

Karen reacted impulsively, in the only way she could to defend herself. Reaching out, she snatched one of Nona's ski poles and wrenched it out of her grip. Swinging wildly, she forced Nona back against the metal rail to avoid the pole's sharp tip.

"You're taking a dive so you might as well go gracefully!'' Brandon shouted up at her. "Don't be a wimp, Nona! *Push* her! Get it over with!''

Cautiously, Nona reached out again. Karen whipped the pole back and forth in front of her to ward Nona off, but Nona wasn't quick enough, and the tip slashed her cheek. A raw, red welt rose to the skin's surface.

Nona let out a pitiful yip of pain and touched her cheek. "Oh, Bran, I'm bleeding!''

"Push her off, damn it!''

For a moment, she hesitated. And Karen dared to hope that she'd refuse to follow her brother's order. Then, with startling speed, Nona's hand shot out and grasped the shaft of the ski pole. She ripped it out of Karen's cold-stiffened fingers, tossing it away. The two girls watched it fall . . . fall . . . fall. . . .

159

The sound of the pole snapping on the rocks below broke through the rising wind.

The two girls stared down in silence. Then Nona's eyes rose to meet hers, and she said, almost kindly, "I'm sorry, Karen. I don't really want to do this but . . ."

With that, Nona kicked the safety bar down and threw herself at Karen. As the bar swung outward, Karen ducked beneath the girl's outstretched arms and reached out to try to bring the metal guardrail back. But by now the quad was rocking so crazily from their struggle that Karen lost her balance, and she felt the cold surface of the chair slipping out from under her as she tumbled forward . . . falling toward the sharp black rocks at the bottom of Devil's Drop.

Chapter 11

Kurt parked in front of the condo and jogged toward the front door. He was tired but relieved that Karen had gone for Mancini—not only for his father's sake, but hers as well. Kurt had learned the hard way that he couldn't trust Brandon, in fact had never really known him. The knowledge that Karen was safely under the protection of the police gave him one less person to worry about. And he was beginning to realize just how important a person she was to him.

He turned the key in the lock and stepped into the living room. "Dad!" he shouted, loping up the stairs toward his father's bedroom. "Dad, you home?"

The room was empty; the bed hadn't been slept in. He tried the next door along the hall—his father's office. Heinz wasn't there either.

"Damn!" he muttered, running a shaky hand through his hair. Where could he have gone at this hour? The Wobbly Barn, his only real hangout, was closed.

Unsure of what to do next, Kurt wandered downstairs and into the kitchen. There he found his father, his head cushioned by one arm on the table, fast asleep.

A Pizza Attack box rested near his arm. It looked as if it hadn't even been opened. Kurt smiled. His Dad hated pizza but knew *he* adored it. This had been meant as a peace offering.

Kurt tapped Heinz gently on the shoulder. "I'm home, Dad."

Slowly, his father straightened up, blinking. "What time is it?"

"Late. Are you still in the mood for pizza? We can nuke it," he said, pointing to the microwave.

"If you'd like to, we can," Heinz said without much enthusiasm.

Kurt laughed. "I'm not very hungry right now. What I really want to do is talk."

And he did. Kurt explained how Matt had died, the innocent victim of the Stewarts' misguided revenge plot.

His father looked shocked. "I feel responsible for your friend's death. I should have told you about the avalanche a long time ago," Heinz whispered mournfully. "I suppose I was afraid of what you'd think of me. You were always so far away, Kurt. At first because your mother wanted it that way. . . . Then, even after you came to live with me, your heart was distant, cold. I couldn't seem to get through to you."

"I'm sorry," Kurt choked out. "It must have been hard." He laid a hand on his father's arm, not able to think of any better way of consoling him.

A soft knock sounded at the kitchen door.

Hoping it was Karen with Mancini, Kurt immediately opened the door. "Jerrie!" he gasped. "What are you doing out at this hour?"

She smiled, purring from deep down in her throat, "I couldn't sleep, babe. So I took myself for a drive, and I just happened to see your light on. It's awful cold out here.''

Kurt was familiar with Jerrie's playful moods, and he didn't have the time or inclination to accommodate her. "Not now, Jerrie."

"Kurt!" she whimpered, sounding hurt. "We have to talk. I want you to understand how special I think you are.'' Her long black hair gleamed under the porch light. "Can I come in?"

Kurt gave his father an apologetic look and stepped outside. Jerrie smiled sweetly at him then eased forward, brushing her right breast against his arm so casually that he might have believed it had happened by accident—if he hadn't known her as well as he did.

"*Jerrie, not now!*" Kurt groaned. "My dad and I—"

"When?" she demanded, standing so close he could feel her breath on his cheek.

But her nearness brought only thoughts of Karen to his mind. Karen with her lovely blond hair, sparkling amber eyes, and warm smile that seemed to light up just for him. "I . . . I don't know," he stammered. "Maybe never."

He backed away from her and reached for the door, but she somehow beat him to the handle. One thing you couldn't deny this girl—she had great reflexes. Jerrie placed a long-fingered hand over the latch.

"Kurt, face it. Things just haven't been the same between us since that New York slut showed up. She's using you to get in with our crowd."

Kurt turned on her, furious, but also amused. "*She* is using me? Come off it, Jerrie. You're the pro at that game. I don't think Karen knows how to use

163

people. She's the nicest girl I've ever known. Now, please move.''

Tears sprang into Jerrie's eyes as she staggered away from Kurt. Her mouth made ugly, silent shapes as if she was trying to keep back a flood of words. They came out anyway. "I . . . I hope Brandon and Nona *do* send her back to New York!" she raged at him.

Kurt stared at her in horror. "What are you talking about?''

Jerrie clamped her mouth shut but looked suddenly smug.

"Tell me!" he demanded.

Coyly, she shrugged one shoulder. "I just happened to overhear Brandon and Nona talking at The Drifts. Something about needing to get rid of Karen. Sounds just fine to me! Pack her off to Manhattan!''

A fresh jolt of fear rocked Kurt. Getting rid of Karen didn't necessarily mean handing her an Amtrak ticket to New York. What if the Stewarts' plans included something more permanent?

He grabbed Jerrie by her arms and shook her hard. "Where are they now?''

At first she appeared pleased with the physical contact, but her lavender eyes rapidly narrowed with concern as Kurt's grip tightened. "How would I know? Hey, that hurts!''

Heinz stepped into the doorway, wearing a concerned expression. "Is everything all right, son?''

Kurt's mind was racing. "No. Brandon's decided he has to get rid of Karen before settling his score with you. Something must have gone wrong with the police, otherwise she would have been here by now.''

"We must find her then," Heinz said solemnly. "Let go of the girl, Kurt." He looked at Jerrie. "Think, my dear. We want no more bloodshed. Was anything said to give you a clue where the Stewarts might be now?''

"I . . . I don't kno-o-ow,'' her voice cracked as she rubbed her arms, casting Kurt a wounded look. ''I guess there was something about Bear Mountain.''

"If Karen has half the sense I think she has, she won't set foot on Bear Mountain.''

On the other hand, he thought with a sinking heart, *she is stubborn and absolutely determined to find Matt's killer. Or killers?* For the first time it occurred to him that Nona might have played as active a part as her brother in Matt's death and the plot to kill Heinz. In that case, the odds were two against one.

"Get your skis,'' Heinz said, as if reading his son's mind. ''We'd better find her fast.''

Karen screamed, wrestling with empty air as the ground spun up toward her. *I'm going to die. I'm going to splatter on those rocks and . . .*

Her outstretched fingers locked around something solid, and she came to a bone-jarring halt. Karen looked up at the quad chair in amazement. She was hanging from the iron safety bar two hundred feet in the air.

"Thank you,'' she whispered hoarsely to whoever passed out second chances in this life.

She closed her eyes and took three shallow breaths to try to clear her head. When she looked around again, two thoughts occurred to her: *The lift is moving, and I am alone in this chair!*

However, she didn't have time to dwell on either fact. The wind was blowing viciously, tugging at her body, making it more and more difficult to hold onto the cold metal. Her gloved fingers slipped by a fraction of an inch with each devilish gust.

Finally, by pulling up, straining every muscle in her arms, Karen managed to swing one leg over the bar. She heaved herself upward far enough to grasp the arm of the chair then struggled back into the seat. Breathing raggedly, she pulled the safety bar into position again and looked along the length of the bench.

Nona was, indeed, gone. A hollow feeling seeped into Karen's stomach, for there was only one place Nona could have gone.

Down.

Glancing back over her shoulder, she could just make out the treacherous black crevice through the blizzard. Nearby, a figure in a yellow ski suit lay sprawled in the snow, one arm flopping weakly as if beckoning for help.

Brandon was bent over Nona, touching her cheek tenderly. For a moment, Karen closed her eyes in relief. At least the girl hadn't hit the rocks. There was a chance she'd survive, having landed in the soft, new snow.

As Karen's chair moved farther up the mountainside, Brandon seemed to shake himself out of his state of shock, and he looked up.

"You bitch!" he yelled, the words echoing off the surrounding mountains. "I'll get you for this . . . for this . . . for this!"

Jumping on the snowmobile again, he started up the slope beneath the lift line, shaking his fist and screaming more obscenities at Karen. She refused to let herself think about what he'd do to her if he caught her. The snowmobile ground away, laboring up the hill with difficulty through deepening drifts. Then she lost sight of Brandon in the blowing snow.

She was cold—colder than she'd ever been in her entire life. Her lips felt as if they'd crack should she try to move them, and her arms ached ferociously from straining to pull herself back up to safety. But she was alive! And the fighter in her refused to give up.

Karen eyed the wooden power shed on the platform above as she approached it. She held her breath, praying, for there was still no sign of Brandon. Maybe he'd flooded out the engine. Maybe the snow was too deep for him to beat her to the top. Once the quad rounded the massive cog wheel, she'd be on her way back down the mountain and would have a chance of reaching her car.

The chair bumped over the cable housing in preparation for its downward trip. She held her breath, squeezing her eyes closed, praying.

Suddenly the lift jerked to a stop. A tremor shot through her body, and slowly, she opened her eyes to face Brandon.

Chapter 12

Brandon glared at her with pure hatred. "Why don't we take a more adventuresome route," he suggested, lowering the lap bar and dragging her out of the chair.

"I . . . I don't have skis," she stammered weakly.

"The ski patrol keeps spares in the power shed."

"I c-can't ski the Fiddle."

He smiled at her wickedly. "That's what I'm counting on, honey."

Then, of course, she knew. Since she'd ruined his plans to kill Haller, he intended to punish her . . . in the most final way possible. And, if he made her death look like an accident, as though she'd recklessly attempted a midnight run down Bear Mountain, no one would ever know. He'd probably even try to convince the police that Nona had fallen while trying to stop her. Kurt would tell a different story, but it would be his word against Brandon's.

"I won't do it!" she insisted.

Brandon slowly lifted his ski pole until the sharp steel point tickled the hollow of her throat. "Either ski with me, or we'll end it here . . . right now."

Karen swallowed back a lump of panic. Time! She

desperately needed time—to think, to allow for Kurt to figure out that something had gone wrong when she didn't show up with the police, to hope against wild hope that Brandon might have a last-minute change of heart.

"I'll ski," she whispered shakily.

He nodded, lowering the pole. "Good choice."

Karen's mind was reeling as Brandon pulled equipment out of the shed with one hand, still holding her tightly with his other. She didn't help him as he lifted her feet out of her shoes, shoving first one then the other into molded ski boots, but she didn't dare resist.

When they were both geared up, he studied her approvingly. "At least you look the part, even though you ski like crap."

"Thanks," she muttered dryly, then glanced down at the necklace lying over her jacket zipper. The opals glowed a seething red. *Why didn't I listen to you?* she thought miserably. *Why?*

Although there had been moments when she'd wished that they possessed the power to warn her of danger, she'd never truly believed in them. Perhaps if she had she wouldn't be in this mess. Her grandmother had believed in their powers and had dared to lead a spectacular life, traveling to exotic and perilous corners of the world under their protection. Karen reached up to caress the smooth glass bauble tenderly, one last time.

"What's that?" Brandon demanded.

Karen looked up at him. "What?"

"That." He tugged on the necklace, and the chain snapped.

The opals seemed to have caught fire, sparking brilliant red and orange in the darkness, their heat so intense Karen imagined she could feel it radiating

170

through the glass globe, even from two feet away. If the stones could have had emotion, she'd say they were enraged by what Brandon was about to do to her.

"Nothing," she murmured sadly, "just a necklace."

Brandon dangled the glowing crimson sphere in front of his eyes. "Weird."

She reached for it. He pulled his hand back. "I don't think you'll be needing jewelry on this trip. Besides, after Nona recovers she might like this as a memento of her old friend." He dropped the necklace into a chest pocket inside his jacket. "Now, let's get going."

Brandon prodded her toward an opening in the trees, which marked the beginning of the Devil's Fiddle.

Her heart pounding, her tongue drying up in her mouth so that she could hardly swallow, Karen surveyed the menacing trail below. Snow was still falling, fast and thick. She could barely see twenty feet ahead of her ski tips.

"No more stalling!" Brandon barked. "Move!" He gave her a firm shove, and she slid over the first drop and onto the wickedly steep run.

Karen immediately assumed her snowplow stance to slow her descent over the icy surface. However, Brandon, skiing beside her, brought his skis into parallel position and glided in tight zigzags with amazing ease.

For the first few minutes he allowed her to take her time, then he slipped behind her. "All right," he shouted against the wind. "Now we race to Devil's Drop. Speed up."

"I can't!" she objected. "If I go any faster, I'll fall."

"You won't fall until I want you to," he growled, moving up still closer behind her.

Brandon gave her a nudge with the grip of his pole, and the muscles in her legs buckled, letting her skis skid out of their safety wedge so that they chattered over the thin new snow and treacherous icy patches. Karen felt as if she were flying—faster and faster, the freezing wind whistling in her ears, slicing viciously into her cheeks. Her eyes burned and watered, nearly blinding her.

This is the last I'll know of this world, she lamented. *Cold . . . crashing down a mountainside . . . sailing off into sub-zero air for a second or two before smashing down onto jagged boulders!*

Karen wondered if there would be much pain, if it would last very long.

But she refused to make her demise any easier on Brandon by giving in to his wishes. Again, she attempted to brake her descent by contracting the muscles in her legs, angling her ski tips inward, trying to locate the fiberglass edges that would bite into the grains of ice. She remembered Matt's lessons, then Kurt's.

"Move, move!" Brandon barked at her back.

He struck her with his pole tip. Then again and again. She heard the sharp metal point rip through her jacket, and on the fourth jab, it stabbed into the flesh between her shoulder blades.

Karen shrieked in pain. She started to lose her balance, but Brandon caught her from behind, shoving her forward. "You aren't stopping now!" he shouted as they barreled down the mountainside. "Just a hundred feet to go!"

A hundred feet to Devil's Drop! Karen's stomach knotted, sensing the awful cliff ahead in the same way she always knew when a roller coaster was gathering speed just before dropping over its highest peak.

Then she caught a flash of motion from the tree line. She turned her head just enough to see two figures skiing toward her at top speed. One skier's aggressive racing form was unmistakable.

Oh Kurt, please! But they were too far away to intercept her and Brandon before they reached the cliff.

"Control the mountain, don't let it control you!" Kurt yelled.

But it was impossible at this speed to revert to her old beginner's style. Instead, she clenched her teeth and hunkered down into a crouch, knees flexed like springs, head tucked against the wind, poles clamped against her sides in her best imitation of the competitors at the Mogul Challenge. If she had to go off a cliff, she'd do it in proper form with the insane prayer that at the end of her plunge she might . . . just might . . . land in one piece on the other side of the rocks.

"No!" Kurt screamed, guessing what she was attempting to do.

I have to, she thought. *There's no other way.*

She was aware of the widening gap between her and Brandon, who must have been surprised by her sudden burst of speed. She heard him repeatedly digging in his poles, pushing off, his skis scraping slalom-style over icy patches, his breath rasping raggedly.

Karen could feel the horrible drop looming just a few feet ahead. In the next second, despite her determination, a paralyzing fear overcame her. She screamed, "Let me off!" just like the time she'd ridden the gargantuan roller coaster at Coney Island.

If you want to stop, just sit down! Matt's earliest coaching advice flashed across her brain.

Karen sat.

She didn't immediately stop but continued to skid toward the precipice. Her poles caught on the branch of a dead bush and were ripped out of her hands. She rolled onto her stomach, scrambling for a handhold on the icy slope, and when a second shadowy shape leapt out of the darkness, she reached out, connected with Kurt's outstretched hand, and held on with every ounce of strength left in her body.

"Aaaah!" Brandon roared.

Karen twisted around, peering up through stinging white flakes, expecting to see him racing toward them full force with both pole tips. But Brandon seemed to be wrestling with his own chest, trying to tear open his jacket, his poles flopping uselessly from their wrist straps. There was a horrified expression of anguish and shock on his face.

He whizzed past—then dropped completely out of sight, leaving behind only a terrible, drawn-out scream that echoed across the six Killington mountains.

At last, there was only silence.

Karen gulped and sat up on the snow beside Kurt, barely a foot away from the cliff's edge, her heart thudding in her ears. Heinz skied to the edge of Devil's Drop and looked over before grimly turning back to face his son.

"It's over," he said.

Tears of relief filled Karen's eyes, and she broke into weary sobs as Kurt's arms came around her.

Chapter 13

The storm cleared by dawn, leaving great loose-powder conditions at Killington and the nearby resorts of Pico, Okemo, and Suicide Six. The lifts were busy, the lines long, and hundreds of recreational skiers were in a festive mood. Only a few expert shredders were disappointed to find that the famous Devil's Fiddle was closed following a strange accident the night before.

At first, as in any small town where unexpected tragedy occurs, gossip ran like wildfire. It was rumored that a local gang of teenagers, drinking heavily, had taken a midnight joy ride on one of the lifts, and a fight had erupted while they were en route to the top. During the struggle, one Killington Regional High student had plummeted from the chair. No one was quite sure of his or her fate.

Within a few days a local weekly newspaper, *The Green Mountain Times*, ran a dramatic article:

ORPHANS' BITTER MEMORIES OF SKIING TRAGEDY
BRING DEATH HOME TO KILLINGTON
In a convoluted plot worthy of a television de-

175

*tective series, a local brother and sister, Brandon
and Nona Stewart, allegedly schemed to avenge
their parents' accidental death fifteen years earlier
in Switzerland. However, their plans backfired.*

*Mistaking fellow high school student Matthew
Welch for their target—local builder Heinz
Haller—they ran young Welch down with the car
of a friend. A month later, during what may have
been a second attempt on Haller's life, the Stewart
girl was seriously injured from a fall off of a chair
lift on Bear Mountain. Brandon Stewart plunged to
his death after skiing over Devil's Drop, a cliff
bordering one of the black diamond trails on Bear
Mountain, not far from where his sister was injured.*

*Nona Stewart suffered two broken legs and a se-
vere concussion from her fall. She remains hospi-
talized.*

*State law officials have released no further in-
formation as to other individuals involved. However, police spokesperson Lieutenant Carl Mancini
promised that further details would be forthcoming.*

It had begun in the Wobbly Barn, and that was where
the kids gathered one Saturday afternoon in late February while the sun warmed the Vermont countryside
and melting icicles dripped from the roof outside the
window of the party room. No one had formally arranged that they should meet. In fact, Lieutenant Mancini had advised each of the teens involved not to
discuss the case with his or her friends until after
Nona's trial for her part in Matt's death and the attempted murder of Karen.

But it was impossible not to talk about it, or to stay
away from one another. They'd been through so much
together—Karen, Kurt, Frank, Rosie, and Jerrie. In

twos or one at a time, they'd arrived, starting sometime around two o'clock. By three they sat on the floor around the fireplace, a huge bowl of nachos smothered with melted cheese and jalapeños in the center of their circle, frosty mugs of root beer in their hands. If a stranger had walked in on them, he might have thought they were having a party. But what they were really doing was revisiting a nightmare in the light of day. It was their way of chasing away the terror—by understanding the truth.

At first they simply sat in silence, listening to the melting ice plunk, plunk, plunk outside the windows.

Finally, Jerrie put down her mug and leaned back on her elbows. "How much longer does Nona have to stay in the hospital?" she asked.

Frank cleared his throat. "Her aunt told me she'll be there at least two more weeks for surgery and physical therapy. After that, she'll go home to her aunt's house to wait for the trial." She had been freed on bail since the judge felt she was unlikely to skip town in her condition.

"Even with treatment, she'll probably have trouble walking without a cane," Rosie commented. "My dad says the nerves in her legs were pretty messed up."

Karen sipped her root beer, then looked around the circle. "I think she'll probably be able to deal with the physical stuff. But . . . living without Brandon . . ." She shook her head. "He was her whole world for so long."

"She'd been willing to do anything for him—even kill," murmured Kurt.

"At least it's finished," said Frank.

Karen nodded, realizing that he was talking about more than the Stewarts' revenge plot. He seemed to have finally accepted the idea that Nona wasn't the girl for him.

Rosie gave Karen an uneasy look. "I'm sure we're all glad it's over. I can't believe you thought I stole your car then accidently killed Matt and tried to cover it up. If I had hit him, I would have run straight to the police and given myself up."

Frank gazed at Rosie with interest. "You would have done that? Turned yourself in?"

"Of course," she said. "I couldn't have lived with the guilt. I'll bet you would have done the same."

Frank nodded. "By the way, sorry to hear about you and your boyfriend at Green Mountain . . . you know, breaking up and all."

Rosie shrugged. "I kept telling him that he was too old for me, but he was so crazy about me he just wouldn't listen."

Karen nearly choked.

Frank nibbled his bottom lip thoughtfully. "I've been considering taking some time off from the restaurant, having more of a social life. Would you like to go to a movie some night?"

Rosie beamed at him. "Sure."

"You were going with a college man?" Jerrie asked, a little late picking up on the conversational thread.

"Yeah." Rosie pulled her wallet out of her purse. "Here's his picture."

Jerrie studied the photo then drew a slow breath and smiled. "He's a hunk. Can I have his phone number?"

"Jerrie!" Karen gasped.

"It's all right," Rosie assured her. "Chuck might like going out with you, Jerrie. He wanted to take me to his fraternity parties, but I could never get permission from my parents."

"Fraternity parties?" Jerrie looked ecstatic at the prospect.

Frank cleared his throat. "Not to change the subject or anything, but there are some things I'm really confused about."

"Like what?" Karen asked.

"Like . . . why Brandon and Nona decided to kill Haller the night of the party." Frank turned to Kurt. "I mean, you and your dad have lived in Killington for years. Why did they wait?"

Kurt considered this for a moment. "I can't remember Brandon meeting my father until about a year ago. When I moved here with Heinz, Brandon and I started hanging out together. But I avoided my father, and since Heinz rarely moved around town much except to walk between the condo, his construction office, and the Wobbly, it was unlikely Brandon would have run into him very often. I suppose that sometime during the past year Brandon must have pulled out the old clippings, which started him thinking about the resemblance. I remember one week when he seemed unusually curious about my family background . . . asked all sorts of questions."

"You weren't suspicious?" Rosie asked.

Kurt shook his head. "Why should I have been? Brandon was just a friend interested in my past."

Karen sighed. "It probably didn't take much to talk Nona into helping him with his plans to kill Heinz." A chill swept up her spine as she recalled the first time she'd met Nona. At that moment, Karen had been convinced the student government president was just being friendly. "Nona admitted that she'd been setting me up all along. I drove to school in my car with out-of-state license plates. She must have thought—man, this is perfect. We'll use her car. If we get away with it—great. But if the police find the car, they'll think this New York chick just couldn't drive in snow, and the car went into a skid.''

Rosie observed her solemnly. "I warned you about how she uses people—but never in a million years did I think she was capable of anything this crazy.''

Karen nodded silently.

"There is one thing I don't understand, though,'' Rosie commented, licking nacho cheese from her fingertips. "How did a beginner like you survive the Fiddle while Brandon, who was practically a pro, skied off the cliff?''

"The autopsy . . .'' Kurt began, his voice taut with emotion, ". . . it showed he'd had a heart attack. But Lieutenant Mancini spoke with Brandon's doctor, and he claims he found nothing in Brandon's most recent physical to indicate he had a heart condition. He was in great shape.''

Karen recalled seeing Brandon clutch his chest just before he pitched over the cliff. But some small detail of that memory didn't quite make sense, and she turned it over and over in her mind for the next hour as the kids talked.

"Kurt,'' she said softly, after the others had left, "before Brandon died, he took my grandmother's necklace, did you—''

Kurt reached into his pocket. "I'm sorry. Lieutenant Mancini gave it to me to return to you. I forgot. Here.''

Karen held her palms open to welcome back the mysterious glass sphere on its gold chain. The opals floated serenely in their clear bath, shining a delicate orchid. *Safe*, she thought. *They're telling me that I'm safe now*.

The opals. Could their changes really be explained by temperature or atmosphere or moods? She no longer believed that was possible, but she was at a loss for a better solution.

For the rest of her life she'd wonder about them . . . and about Brandon's heart attack. Had the seizure that caused him to clutch at his heart been brought on by fear when he realized that he couldn't stop himself from going over the cliff? Had he literally been scared to death? Or had her grandmother's opals, resting in a pocket over his chest, sent a lethal shock into the muscles of his heart, insuring he'd be incapable of saving himself or harming her?

"Thank you," she murmured. *Thank you, Nana.*

"It's all right," Kurt said, assuming her gratitude was intended for him. He put an arm around her, coiling her warmly inside his embrace. With a tender gesture, he lifted her chin and kissed her on the lips.

Karen didn't bother explaining.

Spine-tingling Suspense
from Avon Flare

JAY BENNETT

THE EXECUTIONER   79160-9/$2.95 US/3.50 Can

Indirectly responsible for a friend's death, Bruce is consumed by guilt—until someone is out to get *him*.

CHRISTOPHER PIKE

CHAIN LETTER   89968-X/$3.50 US/$4.25 Can

One by one, the chain letter was coming to each of them... demanding dangerous, impossible deeds. None in the group wanted to believe it—until the accidents—and the dying— started happening!

NICOLE DAVIDSON

WINTERKILL   75965-9/$2.95 US/$3.50 Can

Her family's move to rural Vermont proves dangerous for Karen Henderson as she tries to track down the killer of her friend Matt.

CRASH COURSE   75964-0/$2.95 US/$3.50 Can

A secluded cabin on the lake was a perfect place to study...or to die.

TERRIFYING TALES OF
SPINE-TINGLING SUSPENSE

THE MAN WHO WAS POE   Avi
71192-3/$3.50 US/$4.25 Can
Is the mysterious stranger really the tormented writer
Edgar Allan Poe, looking to use Edmund's plight as the
source of a new story—with a tragic ending?

DYING TO KNOW   Jeff Hammer
76143-2/$2.95 US/$3.50 Can
When Diane Delany investigates the death of her sworn
enemy, she uncovers many dark secrets and begins to
wonder if she can trust anyone—even her boyfriend.

FIELD TRIP   Jeff Hammer
76144-0/$2.99 US/$3.50 Can
On a weekend field trip, Tom Martin doesn't know who
to turn to when students start disappearing, leaving
behind only their blood-spattered beds.

ALONE IN THE HOUSE   Edmund Plante
76424-5/$2.99 US/$3.50 Can
In the middle of the night Joanne wakes up all alone...
almost.

ON THE DEVIL'S COURT   Carl Deuker
70879-5/$2.99 US/$3.50 Can
Desperate for one perfect basketball season, Joe Faust will
sacrifice anything for triumph... even his soul.